D0290710

1930

THE
LOBO
BREED

**Center Point
Large Print**

**This Large Print Book carries the
Seal of Approval of N.A.V.H.**

THE
LOBO
BREED

CHARLES M. MARTIN

CENTER POINT PUBLISHING
THORNDIKE, MAINE

This Center Point Large Print edition
is published in the year 2009 by arrangement with
Golden West Literary Agency.

The text of this Large Print edition is unabridged.
In other aspects, this book may vary
from the original edition.
Printed in the United States of America.
Set in 16-point Times New Roman type.

ISBN: 978-1-60285-525-0

Library of Congress Cataloging-in-Publication Data

Martin, Chuck.
  The lobo breed / Charles M. Martin.
    p. cm.
  ISBN 978-1-60285-525-0 (library binding : alk. paper)
  1. Large type books. I. Title.

PS3525.A7455L6 2009
813'.54--dc22

2009012511

CHAPTER ONE

Gospel Cummings raised his head slightly with an inquiring expression in his narrowed brown eyes. His bearded face was lined with tell-tale furrows, the marks of character which only the sure years of experience bring to a man.

Something was moving outside the tight little cabin which occupied a small island of land at the intersection of Three Points. A friend would have announced his presence; the badlands in the near distance were a haven for outlaws.

The gaunt plainsman listened intently for a long moment. Then he spoke quietly, but with stern authority.

"Come out from cover and enter in peace, my friend!"

There was silence for a time; a silence which was natural in the vicinity of Hell's Half Acre, of which Gospel Cummings was the self-appointed caretaker. The living had to care for the dead, and Cummings earned a precarious livelihood by reading a simple service over the graves of those who died with their boots on.

A boot scuffed on the gravel just outside the cabin door. Gospel Cummings half turned, eyes alert, but his big frame thoroughly relaxed. He had seen them come and go, the wanted men of the badlands and the wild young cowboys who rode back to join the owl-hoot clan from time to time. His bearded lips moved briefly as he spoke again.

"Enter!"

The door opened slowly. A tall lean cowboy crouched forward with a cocked six-shooter in his grimy right fist. His narrowed blue eyes held the look of the hunted, but his square jaw told of a determination out of keeping with the number of his years.

Gospel Cummings glanced at the shadow which spiked across his freshly scrubbed plank floor. His brown eyes lighted with recognition. Again he spoke softly, his deep voice warm and friendly.

"Howdy, Jeff; holster your smoke-pole and fix yourself a bait of grub. You look kinda peaked."

The lean cowboy swayed back as he caught his breath sharply. But the gun in his hand did not waver.

"You know me?" he asked in a strained, husky whisper.

Cummings nodded. "Seen you many's the time back on Lobo's Peak," he answered. "I'm not at war with you or your Pa, like he might have told you. There's beef stew on the back of the stove."

"You're friends with that hulkin' law-dog name of Saint John," the young cowboy grated. "And there's a price on the Lobo's scalp like you know!"

"I'm no bounty hunter, son," Cummings said with quiet dignity. "I am a simple man of peace."

Jeff Dawson sheathed his six-shooter and moved across the room. He took a bowl from the table and ladled stew from the simmering pot on the back of the stove, but all the while his eyes watched for any hostile move from his host.

"Sit down and rest," Cummings suggested. "Why did the Lobo send you down to Three Points to make medicine with me?"

Once again Jeff Dawson palmed his six-shooter, "How'd you know that?" he demanded.

"You wouldn't have come this close to town unless the need was urgent," Cummings answered.

"I got a mind to kill you, you old sin-buster," the cowboy threatened hoarsely. "Like as not you was riding with that crowd of glory-hunters that bushed me and the Lobo over near Lost River!"

Gospel Cummings did not smile: His glance touched the open pages of the old Bible on the deal table before him, and then he shook his head.

"I'm allowing you one mistake, yearling," he said bluntly. "Now you listen close while I make talk. I'm not a man of the cloth, and I'm not a part of the law. As for killing me, 'Thou shalt not kill!' The Book says so."

"How'd you know the Lobo was hurt?" Dawson asked more quietly. "How'd you know he sent me down here to make medicine with you?"

"You're here, and bad news travels fast," Cummings retorted. "I saw the Boyd boys ride

7

past not long since; Tom said there would be a service to read over a new grave. Looks like he was wrong."

A spasm of grief twisted the young face of Jeff Dawson. He stood up, an even six feet, wide through the shoulders and not yet fully filled out. "There'll be more than *one* service!" he promised bitterly. "The Lobo ain't rightly an outlaw, and he's tough. He'll take a lot of killing!"

"Spoken like a man," Cummings agreed gruffly. "We raise our cow-fellers tough in these parts. Now suppose you tell your part of it so's I will know what Tom Boyd meant."

"Them Boyds was right, Gospel," Jeff Dawson said in a choked voice. "The Lobo ain't long for this world. He wants to talk to you before he crosses over to the big Green Pastures. You'll ride with an owl-hooter this one time?"

"I'd ride with the Devil if I could do him any good," Gospel Cummings said grimly. "But you ain't no owl-hooter, Jeff."

"No?" Dawson said bitterly. "It was Terry Boyd who shot Dad on a sneak, and it was me who evened up for the Lobo!"

Cummings said thoughtfully, "Looks like you're a chip off the old block. Wait here a minute and eat your grub while I saddle old Fred, my sorrel."

"Then you'll ride back with me?" Dawson asked eagerly. "To talk to the Lobo before he cashes in his chips?"

"I'll ride. I never did believe that Jim Dawson held up Tom Boyd and stole that 3 B payroll," Cummings answered. "I'll be with you in a matter of minutes."

Jeff Dawson relaxed and began to eat the savory stew. He did not glance around when a boot scuffed on the door-sill. Then he glanced idly at the shadow spiking across the worn floor. His right hand started for his worn holster, but a stern voice spoke sharply.

"Leave the hardware ride, younker. The law speaking, and I've got you covered!"

"That lying old Holy Joe!" Dawson said bitterly. "He told me he was no part of the law!"

John Saint John was a big man, and what law there was in Vaca town. He also had the big man's arrogance, but his prognathous jaw marked him as a man of courage. His hard mouth was framed by a pair of cowhorn mustaches which twitched when he spoke.

"I didn't see Gospel," the big deputy growled. "But I did see you, and I'm taking you for the law!"

The big deputy sheriff reached for a pair of handcuffs at the back of his belt. A gun-barrel thudded down heavily on his head, and Saint John slumped to the floor with a little grunt.

Gospel Cummings caught the falling officer and said sharply to the staring cowboy, "Make a run for the Devil's Graveyard and get your hoss! Meet

9

me up on the trail where it branches to the bad-lands, and don't stand there staring like a fool pil-grim!"

Jeff Dawson ran from the cabin and disappeared in the brush. Gospel Cummings sighed and reached into the right tail of his black broadcloth coat. His hand came out holding a quart bottle of Three Daisies whiskey, and after drawing the cork with his teeth, the gaunt plainsman drank deeply. Then, reaching under his bunk, Cummings took a full quart of whiskey and placed it in the right tail of his coat, on the side where the badman of his nature had its abode. That was also the side on which he carried his heavy forty-five Peacemaker Colt six-shooter.

The tall plainsman was a man with a dual per-sonality, and he made no attempt to conceal this fact from those he called friends. None had ever seen him under the influence of strong drink, but none could remember seeing him without the quart of Three Daisies in the right tail pocket of his coat. He admitted that strong drink was his besetting sin. Other men stole horses or bullied lesser men. Each had his faults, and Gospel Cummings judged none of them. If they judged him, it was seldom in his presence.

He closed the Bible and dropped it in the left tail of his long coat, on the side where the good man of his nature lived. He took another drink for the road, placed the half-emptied bottle close to the right hand of the unconscious deputy, and left the cabin.

His hip-shot sorrel was standing at the tie-rail, and Cummings mounted expertly. He rode his horse for an hour before leaving the broad trail that led on to Cole Brighton's Box B spread and Ace Fleming's Circle F. The trail to the west led to the badlands, and to the Utah trail. Cummings studied the ground and nodded. He glanced at the trail side brush and read the sign. He reined to a stop near a copse of lodge-pines, and spoke quietly.

"Ride out, Jeff; I'm traveling alone!"

Jeff Dawson rode out of the brush, holstering his six-shooter with a shamed grin. He was straddling a deep-chested Morgan horse; a dark bay with black points.

"Sorry I mistrusted you, old-timer," he apologized to Cummings. "I can't figure out why you even bothered."

"Mebbe I'm my brother's keeper," Cummings said dryly.

"You're in bad with the law now," Dawson said slowly. "You'll pard up with me?"

"In bad? Look, cowboy," Cummings explained patiently. "In this land of the free a man is considered innocent until he is proven guilty. He don't have to convict himself. Saint John don't know who cold-cocked him, and he never will unless the only feller who saw it gives up head and goes around shooting off his mouth!"

"You should have been a law-sharp, Gospel," Dawson said, and his admiration was sincere and boyish. "I'll never tell."

"Then he'll never know for sure," Cummings growled. "Saint John is a good man, and a square peace officer. He's an awful lot of man, like you know. You keep out of the Saint's way from now on, until we clear old Jim's good name!"

"Clear Hades with a grubbing hoe!" Jeff Dawson said viciously. "My Dad has been riding outside the law a long time, like we both know. He's fair game for any sneaking hero who wants to shoot him down from cover. And he was shot down on a sneak," he added bitterly.

"It still don't make old Jim guilty," Gospel Cummings insisted. "It might take considerable time to clear old Jim, but the world wasn't made in a day!"

Jeff Dawson smiled coldly in the fading twilight.

"They've branded old Jim a rustler," he said bitterly. "And if you did clear his name, what good would that do a dead man?"

Cummings answered promptly, "A man lives through his get, and you're old Jim's only chip. If we clear his name, you can start life as an honest man!"

"Not while those Boyds are alive," Dawson said angrily. "But mebbe they won't live too long!"

"Look, yearling," Cummings warned sharply. "I'm not riding with you to aid and abet an owl-hooter. I've always rode on the right side of the law, and I always will."

"I carry what law I need in my holster," Dawson said. "Those Boyd hombres have branded me and the Lobo as owl-hooters, and now there will be a price on my scalp. I mean to look after myself!"

"Thou shalt not kill!" Cummings warned sternly. "He who lives by the sword, shall die by the sword!"

"I'm just twenty," Jeff Dawson said quietly. "Billy the Kid was only twenty-one when he was rubbed out, but he killed twenty-one men before he died!"

Gospel Cummings stopped his horse and faced the grim-faced young outlaw. Dawson stopped his Morgan automatically, his right hand hovering above the holstered pistol on his thigh.

"I've seen most things once, and some of them twice," Cummings said slowly. "Life don't owe me much, but yours is all ahead of you. I dunno," he said slowly. "I'm sure I can beat you to the gun. If I do, it might save a lot of needless bloodshed!"

"Speak with a single tongue," the youth flashed back angrily. "I'll try to hold up my end!"

"You'd only try," Cummings said slowly.

Dawson growled, "I don't have to take slack-jaw from any hombre who crowds my trail!"

"I've got you faded," Cummings repeated. "I'm faster than you are, but you learn the hard way, seems as though!"

"A man can't die but one time!" Dawson retorted. "If that's the way you want it, turn loose your wolf!"

"Uh, uh," Cummings said quietly. "I only shoot in self-defense. Then I never kill the other feller. But I'm warning you, Jeff Dawson. You draw on me again, and you won't ever trigger another killer slug!"

Jeff Dawson laughed without mirth. "Thou shalt not kill!" he scoffed.

"I never kill," Cummings repeated.

Jeff Dawson widened his eyes. "You mean you'd cripple me for life?" he whispered.

"So help me!" Cummings promised.

Jeff Dawson stared into the deep-set brown eyes, at the strong, bearded face of this strange man with the dual personality. There was no fear in Dawson's mind, but gradually the anger drained from him and left him what he was—a weary young boy who had not yet attained his full growth.

"I'll pass for now," he whispered. "The Lobo needs us both; we can settle this thing some other time!"

"Not so," Cummings said sternly. "We'll settle it now, Jeff. You can't ever escape from anything by running away from it. Well?"

"Blast you, you old sin-buster!" Dawson burst out. "Fill your hand and come out a-smoking!"

"Uh, uh," Cummings said, with a shake of his

head. "After you, and I'll play what I catch on the draw. I'm waiting!"

"I don't need an edge!" Dawson growled, and there was a raspy edge in his voice. "Even-steven is good enough for me, and if I lose, I might take you along to make it a draw!"

"It wouldn't be a draw," Cummings said quietly.

His deep voice was low and quiet, and there was no look of boastfulness in his brown eyes or deeply-lined face. Just a calm statement of facts, gleaned from a lifetime of gun-smoke experience.

Jeff Dawson crouched over in his saddle. Gospel Cummings sat tall and straight, with a deep seat. There was no emotion visible on his bearded face, but there was a slight tremble in his hands.

"I'm waiting," he repeated softly.

Dawson stared with his left hand clenched. Then he lowered his head and raised both hands shoulder high.

"I know when I'm beat," he admitted in a whisper. "You talk, and I'll listen to your wau-wau!"

Cummings nudged his horse a step closer and offered his right hand. "You've won a big victory, Jeff," he said earnestly. "I'm offering you the right hand of friendship, and I'll help you all I can. All I want is for you to be guided some by my judgment. If that judgment gets you in trouble, I'll fight to help you out of it."

Jeff Dawson shot out his hand and gripped hard. Gospel Cummings vised down savagely to find expression for the emotions which now seethed through his veins like an angry, pent-up flood.

"I want you to know, Jeff," Cummings said earnestly: "A man can't do his best fighting when he is wrong. Now you get a brace on yourself while I walk my horse back here in the bresh a way to take a look at my saddle. Don't follow me!"

He whirled old Fred and rode deep into the sage and creosote bush. He dismounted stiffly with his back to the horse's head. His right hand darted into the cavernous pocket of his coat; came out clutching the full quart of Three Daisies. It had been thus for more than twenty years. Whenever his swift hand felt the urge for a speedy draw, the physical reaction from holding his anger in check brought another weakness to the fore. There had been long years when he had promised himself to conquer his weakness. Gospel Cummings sighed softly. He had long since given up that high resolve.

Now his brown hands were steady, but a brooding look of sorrow lurked deep in his eyes when he mounted his horse and rode back to join the cowboy who waited in the murky gloom.

"You get that saddle fixed?" Dawson asked quietly.

"I got it fixed," Cummings answered with quiet dignity. "Where abouts did you leave old Jim?"

"In a cave close to Lost River," Dawson answered in a muffled voice. "I'll warn you now, Gospel. Don't go trying to break a trail into Beulah land for the Lobo. It won't do you a mite of good. He ain't a bit repentant, and you won't need the Scriptures!"

"If I can't bend the lead for old Jim, mebbe so I can bring up the drag and close the gate after him," Cummings answered in trail-talk. "How bad is he hurt?"

Jeff Dawson swayed forward, both hands gripping his saddle-horn. His thin face twisted with a hatred he made no effort to control. Gospel Cummings got part of his answer before young Dawson spoke.

"They bush-whacked old Jim!" Dawson ground out. "Shot him from the bresh without giving the old man a mite of chance!"

"They?" Cummings repeated after Dawson. "You mean more than one of them blasted old Jim?"

"Terry Boyd was the one," Dawson admitted slowly. "And I hope the sneaking killer is kicking up hot ashes right now. Tom Boyd wasn't in on the bushing; I'll give him that much. But he rode out there with the others, and it was them Boyds who put a frame on old Jim!"

"You still didn't tell me how bad that old cow-feller was hurt," Cummings said.

"Too bad," Dawson answered bluntly. "He's

17

taken a 45 slug high in the left breast, just above the heart. I packed him back into the cave, plugged the hole as best I could, and made him easy. He wanted to see you, so I set out to fetch you."

"So time's a-wasting," Cummings growled. "Hit a high lope and let's get long gone!"

Jeff knew that Cummings was familiar with every trail and hideout in the lava badlands. Without more talk, the young cowboy touched his Morgan with the spurs and went racking away through the brush. Old Fred kept right on the Morgan's heels, and both horses were lathered when Dawson rode up a narrow brush-choked trail that led to a large cave.

"Light down and go to him," Dawson whispered brokenly. "I'll take care of the horses. And, Gospel!"

"Yeah, Jeff?"

"Go easy on old Jim," Jeff pleaded, and now he seemed like a very young boy. "He's all I've got, and he ain't in no shape to take a tongue-whipping!"

"Which same I never do," Cummings said gently. "I've known your Dad a heap of years, Jeff. I know he is just as honest as the day is long. Circumstances were against him, just like they are for every man some time in his life. You don't have to be ashamed that you are kin to Jim Dawson."

CHAPTER TWO

Long shadows slanted across the badlands as Gospel Cummings climbed the steep trail leading to the mouth of the brush-choked cave. The gaunt plainsman's heart was heavy as he remembered Jeff Dawson's description of his father's wound.

Gospel Cummings heard a voice call a challenge from the dark interior of the cave.

"Who comes? Speak up fast!"

"It's Gospel Cummings, Jim," the plainsman answered quickly. He knew that a man who had been hunted as long as Jim Dawson would shoot first, and Dawson would shoot straight.

"Come in, Gospel," the wounded man answered wearily. "Been waiting for you."

Cummings hurried his steps and entered the cave. He stopped for a time until his eyes had become accustomed to the gloom of the cave, and then he moved forward.

Jim Dawson was waiting, his back against his bedroll. The tall, slender outlaw looked like a man of sixty. A stubbled beard covered the lower part of his jaw, and his sunken eyes were closed. He opened them slowly as a heavy rifle came up in his thin brown hands. Then Jim Dawson smiled and lowered the rifle with a sigh.

"Howdy, Gospel," he said weakly. "I knew you'd come, old friend!"

Gospel Cummings sat down on a blanket and took the wounded man's right hand. He did not speak for a time; his eyes were studying the scars of the owl-hoot years on the face of his old friend.

"You ain't but forty-two, Jim," Cummings whispered. "I recall when you were a lot like young Jeff. You came to make a hand on the old XIT spread down there in Texas!"

"That was a thousand years ago," Dawson said with a wan smile. "How's Sandra?"

"She's well, and she'll be proud you asked about her," Cummings answered slowly.

"Fine gal, Sandra Fleming," the outlaw murmured. "You've been like a father to her."

"I might have been her father, if things had been different," Cummings admitted. "Sandra's mother was the only girl I ever loved."

"So you never did marry," Dawson murmured, and his voice was that of a man who talks to avoid a more serious matter.

"I never did," Cummings agreed. "But that was down in Texas, Jim. This is high Arizona. I've been happier since Sandra came over here and married Ace Fleming. They make a fine couple."

"You should have married her Ma," Dawson insisted. "She loved you, and her father wanted you for a partner in the best cattle spread in Texas."

"I never did conquer my besetting sin," Cummings admitted quietly, and reached for the bottle in the right tail of his long coat. "Jeff says you was bit by a side-winder. Take a snort of this snake-bite to keep up your strength. You wanted to talk some, remember?"

He pulled the cork with his teeth and held the bottle to Jim Dawson's pallid lips. The wounded outlaw drank deeply, and sighed with appreciation. Then Gospel Cummings raised the bottle to his own bearded lips.

"To the confusion of our enemies, Jim," he made a toast. "You was saying?"

"It won't be long now, Gospel," the wounded outlaw answered, but now his voice was stronger. "I never lifted that 3 B payroll like them Boyds allowed. On top of that, I never rustled any of their beef, except for camp meat. And that ain't all. Terry Boyd shot me on a sneak, without giving me a chance!"

"I know," Cummings murmured. "Jeff was telling me about it."

"Jeff evened the score some," Dawson said proudly. "He will even it some more before them Boyds wipe out the last of the Dawsons!"

A frown crossed the bearded face of Gospel Cummings.

"Jeff is only a yearling, Jim. He ain't got his full growth, and it don't seem right for him to get a start off on the wrong foot!"

"They gave a dog a bad name," Dawson growled. "Just like they did to me. So help me, Gospel, I never robbed the 3 B outfit!"

"That's good enough for me, Jim," Cummings answered. "Why didn't you come in and stand trial?"

Jim Dawson laughed shortly. I didn't have a chance," he said slowly. "I'd have got ten years in the pen as shore as shootin'. I knew I'd never live ten years shut away from the sun, so I just stayed back in the badlands and lived free while I could!"

"Three long years," Cummings murmured. "The Saint never tried hard to find you."

A frown crossed his bearded face as Cummings thought of Saint John. He shrugged irritably, tightened his lips, and waited for Dawson to speak.

"I had two sections of land back there by the 3 B," Dawson began slowly. "It's gone now on account of the taxes."

"Wrong," Cummings contradicted. "Your friends paid the taxes every year."

"Ace Fleming," Dawson said thoughtfully. "Ace is a square gambler, but he took my little Triangle D herd, I was just getting a good start!"

"Ace took the herd," Cummings admitted. "He sold off the steers, and kept the young stuff in your brand. Ace figured young Jeff would need a start one of these days, and the cattle and money are waiting whenever Jeff makes up his mind to come out of the bresh."

"You mean Ace Fleming did that for me?" Dawson whispered.

"There's four thousand in cash for Jeff when he's twenty-one," Cummings answered. "And a nice foundation herd of better than three hundred critters."

"You'll side my chip, Gospel, old pard?" the wounded outlaw pleaded. "Help him to be an honest man?"

"That's the main reason I rode back here," Cummings admitted. "I want Jeff to be honest, like his father always has been. There are others who want to help Jeff; he won't be a lone wolf, Jim!"

Jim Dawson's face clouded. "The Lobo's whelp," he whispered. "Jeff is the son of the old wolf!"

"There's a difference," Cummings argued slowly. "Jeff ain't of age as yet, and he will have plenty of friends on the outside."

"Can I count on that?" Jim Dawson asked weakly. "You'll side him while he makes his fight to make a go of it on the Triangle D?"

"Count it done, Jim," Cummings promised. His face clouded again. "Can you tell me why the Boyds want those two sections of yours so bad?" he asked.

"How long have the Boyds been in Arizona?" Dawson countered.

"Matter of about four years."

"You ever hear of the James boys?"

"Who hasn't?" Cummings answered tartly.

"There was a yarn about the James boys hiding about a hundred thousand in loot," Dawson answered. "Course it's stolen money, but there was also said to be a pile of diamonds and jewelry."

"You never ran with the James boys," Cummings stated bluntly. "What's all this palaver got to do with you and the Boyds?"

"That loot is some place on the Triangle D," Dawson said. "The Boyds know it, though I can't tell you how they found out."

"A hundred thousand is a lot of money," Cummings said thoughtfully. "It must have been from that last big raid when the James boys held up the Katy Flyer down there in the Nations. I know the loot never was recovered by the law."

"Yeah, the law," Dawson said bitterly. "They didn't do much of a job of catching a gang of out-laws, so they put an honest man on the dodge!"

"I know how you feel, old friend," Cummings agreed quietly. "But right now we've got to think about young Jeff. All of his life is ahead of him."

Dawson's anger seemed to give him strength. "Jeff shot that sneaking Terry Boyd, and they will be out to get him!"

"If they do, I'll square the tally, Jim," Cummings promised earnestly. "I figure most times that a growed man can look after himself, but Jeff ain't rightly what you'd call a growed man."

Dawson leaned back with a sigh of satisfaction.

"Jeff couldn't have a better saddle-pard," he said slowly. "And I don't want him to get mixed up with that outlaw loot!"

"You found it?" Cummings asked quickly.

"I never found it," Dawson admitted. "One night about three years ago, an old buscadero rode into the Triangle D on a spavined horse. This old jasper was wounded about the way I'm shot up now. He said three brothers had tried to make him talk; had shot him when he made a fast getaway one night."

"What for kind of hoss was this old he straddling?" Cummings asked.

"It was a 3 B hoss," Jim Dawson murmured. "He didn't last long, this old saddle-bum. Said he was one of the James gang."

"Yeah, I know," Cummings said with a nod. "He died that night, and I read a prayer over his grave back there in the Devil's Graveyard."

"That money is some place on the Triangle D," Dawson said in a whisper. "There's an old cave between two small hills where a waterfall used to be. The bandits buried the loot and set off dynamite to make a slide over the face of the cave. They were all killed or captured except old Fred Haney, which wasn't this jasper's right name."

"So all you had to do was find that old cave."

"I hunted for six months, and then I was framed for that 3 B hold-up," Dawson said bluntly. "I never did find the place, but Jeff is still young.

Keep him straight, Gospel, and help him get a start!"

"Here's my hand on it, Jim!" Cummings promised. "Fifteen hundred acres ain't much of a cattle spread, but it's a heap of land for to go looking for a needle in a haystack!"

"I've got no proof, but add it all up," Dawson whispered, and now his voice was growing weaker. "Old Haney said three brothers had tried to make him talk, and they shot him. He was straddling a 3 B hoss, and the Boyds wanted my little outfit. They framed me for a hold-up I never did, and now they've done for me. You've got to side my chip Gospel!"

"I've often wondered," Cummings muttered. "About that old question we read in the Scriptures. 'Am I my brother's keeper?' If I was to look on Jeff as a younger brother, I could mebbe so keep him honest."

"He don't lack for sand," Jim Dawson murmured weakly. "You'll find that Jeff will do to take along!"

Gospel Cummings nodded agreement. That one little phrase was the highest compliment one cowboy could pay another. *He'll do to take along!*

"That makes up my mind for me, Jim," Cummings told the wounded man, and now his strong hands were trembling.

There was silence for a while, and then a hollow

rattle broke the stillness. In an instant Gospel was beside the stricken man. Gospel Cummings stared at the pale bearded face for a long moment. He reached out a hand and gently closed the dead man's staring sightless eyes. Running boots warned him, and Cummings turned just as Jeff Dawson ran to his father.

"How is he, Gospel?" the cowboy whispered. "You think he'll make it?"

Gospel Cummings nodded. "He's already made it, Jeff," he said gently. "Old Jim has taken the long trail into that far away land from whose bourne no traveler ever returns!"

"You mean he's . . . gone West?" Jeff whispered harshly.

Cummings nodded. "I'll leave you with him for a time."

Jeff Dawson took his father's hand and sat down beside the body. Gospel Cummings stretched to his feet, scooped up the bottle of Three Daisies surreptitiously, and walked to the front of the cave.

Cummings closed his eyes and leaned against the side of the cave. His thoughts traversed the memory trail of more than a quarter of a century, when he and Jim Dawson had made working hands on the old XIT spread down in Texas. Life had been good for both of them then, and both had been rated as top hands.

Cummings turned slowly when dragging spurs

chimed on the rocky floor of the cave. Jeff Dawson had two gun-belts strapped around his lean hips. His young face was a mask of savage determination.

"I'm getting about my snake-hunting, Gospel. Them Boyds killed old Jim, and he was the onliest kin I had. My Ma died when I was nine, and I aim to square up for the old man!"

"You figure you can do it better with two six-shooters?"

"There's two of them Boyds left," Jeff Dawson answered thickly. "I aim to get 'em both!"

"Let's set a spell," Cummings suggested. "You can't go chousing off on your snake-killing, not until old Jim is put away proper. Now can you, cowboy?"

Jeff Dawson clenched his hands and ground a high boot-heel into the rocky floor. "Blast you, Gospel!" he raged. "You know I can't ride out and leave old Jim a-layin' there!"

"So we'll sit and make medicine," Cummings answered. "We'll take Jim back to town and have Boot Crandall fix him up nice. I'll read the service, and you stay right with me until it is all over!"

"Can't do it, Gospel," Jeff Dawson said fiercely. "That law-dog would pick me up sure, and those Boyds would sign the complaint!"

"Mebbe not," Cummings said quietly. "Right now they have troubles of their own."

"And they will figure I made those troubles," Jeff said with savage satisfaction. "I'm not sorry!"

Gospel Cummings studied the angry face of his young companion. "Sometimes a feller can avoid trouble by thinking ahead," he suggested. "If he thinks about what his actions will bring him, sometimes it stops him from acting rash before he acts!"

"I've done acted," Jeff Dawson growled. "I'm not sorry!"

"It does things to a man to have blood on his hands," Cummings said thoughtfully. "He's taken something he can't give back!"

"Mebbe he wouldn't want to give it back if he could," Dawson argued hoarsely.

"You didn't kill a man," Cummings said quietly.

"What did you say?"

"I said you never killed Terry Boyd," Cummings repeated. "Your slug creased his scalp and knocked him down. Matter of fact, Tom and Dixon Boyd don't know who took that long shot at their brother."

Jeff Dawson seized Cummings by the right hand. "Are you just saying that to get me to the burying?" he asked.

Gospel Cummings shook his head. "Uh, uh," he answered. "I was talking to Terry Boyd myself. As for Saint John, he was exceeding his authority when he threw down on you. He didn't have any warrant, and there's no complaint against you.

When old Jim took out on the long trail, he really gave you your freedom!"

Jeff Dawson sucked in a long deep breath. "I can ride and talk with honest men again," he murmured, and then his face hardened. "So the first thing I'll do after the service is sketch me three snakes. I won't miss next time!"

"You've got a lot to live for," Cummings said carelessly. "A nice little cattle spread, about three hundred head of cattle, and money in the bank. All you've got to do is behave like a man until you are twenty-one years old. That's about four months more. You going to throw it all away?"

"Yeah!" Dawson snarled. "I'm gonna throw it all away to square up for my Dad. Them Boyds ain't fitten to live, and I mean to see that they don't!"

"Let's see," Cummings said musingly. "If Saint John knowed that it was you who creased Terry Boyd, he could take you in for assault with a deadly weapon!"

"That's right," Dawson agreed with a grim smile. "And if that big deputy knowed it was you who hit him with the barrel of a hog-leg, he could gather you into the fold for the same reason!"

"Hmmm, you've got a point there," Cummings admitted.

"So I'll get on with my snake-killing after the service," Jeff Dawson announced firmly.

"Seems like I was talking just to get the wind off my belly," Cummings said with a sigh.

"Yeah, and then there are promises," Jeff said simply. "Like the one I made to old Jim not long ago."

Gospel Cummings frowned and screwed up his eyes. He seemed to be struggling with a problem, and then his face cleared.

"Ace Fleming banked your money for you, Jeff," he began again. "He also saved out the young stuff to give you a foundation herd. The taxes are paid on the Triangle D, and when you have reached your majority, you will be a man of substance."

"Square feller, Ace Fleming is," Dawson said gratefully. "He's another hombre who always keeps his promises!"

"I made old Jim a promise, too, just before he breathed his last," Cummings said slowly. "Said I'd look after his chip, and try to make him an upright and honest man. I aim to keep that promise if I have to kill old Jim's chip to do it!"

Jeff Dawson made a derisive sound with his pursed lips. "Hogwash," he sneered. "Thou shalt not kill. Remember?"

Gospel Cummings sighed and shook his wide shoulders. "Look, Jeff," he pleaded. "That's twice within ten minutes that you've outsmarted me. Now why in tarnation don't you use your mind to beat them Boyd brothers, and square up legal for old Jim at the same time?"

"Name me one reason why I should," Jeff Dawson replied.

"Keep your hands away from your hardware, son," Cummings warned. "That one reason is . . . Connie Brighton!"

Jeff Dawson stiffened and then leaped at Gospel Cummings. The gaunt plainsman met the attack and threw the lean cowboy hard with a flying mare. Then he sat on Jeff Dawson's heaving chest and threatened him with a rocky fist.

"You act up any more like a pilgrim, I aim to lower the boom on you," Cummings threatened. "Connie is much too good for the likes of you, but she still thinks you are the finest boy in the world, which you ain't!"

"The devil I ain't!" Jeff Dawson shouted, and then he grinned slowly and offered his right hand. "You're the best, you old sin-buster, and no offense," he said slowly. "Roll off my chest so I can breathe again."

Cummings rolled over and jerked Jeff to his feet with a comradely tug. They stood looking at each other with new respect, and then Jeff Dawson slowly removed his battered old gray Stetson.

"Saying I'm sorry, old friend," he whispered humbly. "Losing my head in the presence of the deceased. You made old Jim a promise, and if I'm just half the man he was, I'll help you keep it."

"Spoke like a man, Jeff," Cummings praised him heartily. "Sometimes a boy grows up sudden overnight. You've done it."

"Jim Dawson was as honest as the day is long,"

Jeff said reverently. "He never did that stick-up job on the 3 B payroll!"

"That was all part of a scheme," Cummings agreed. "Jim had it pretty well figured out, but he didn't live long enough to prove it. Now say you go getting yourself killed; there won't be any point in trying to clear old Jim's good name. Will there?"

"No point," Jeff admitted. "Why did the Boyds want our little old run-down Triangle D spread?"

"Because there's a heap of treasure buried there somewhere," Cummings answered without hesitation. "Some old *banditto* said he had belonged to the James gang, and they buried the treasure in a cave on the Triangle D!"

"I remember that old mossyhorn," Dawson said slowly. "Come to think of it, he was shot up the same way Jim was."

Gospel Cummings narrowed his brown eyes as he stroked his silky beard. He nodded as though he had made a discovery of importance. "Whoever shot old Fred Haney made one little mistake," Cummings announced. "He can't call his shots so good, and he pulls a mite high off center!"

Jeff leaned forward, his nostrils dilated. "I know who shot Jim," he said hoarsely. "It was Terry Boyd. He's got a cast in his left eye!"

"The law will take care of Terry Boyd in time," Cummings said soothingly. "You don't want to do anything to put yourself a-straddle of the owl-hoot again. Your Dad was only forty-two, and you see what it did to him."

"Look, Gospel," Jeff Dawson said earnestly. "I'm going to give the law a fair chance. If it doesn't work, I'll use my own kind of law. You made Jim a promise; now I'm making you one!"

Gospel Cummings nodded sadly. Jeff was a chip off the old block, and Jim Dawson was a man of his word. He had also been a man of courage, but the brightest courage in the world could not stand up against bush-whack lead.

"Fair enough, pard," Cummings said to the cowboy. "Now you listen to me. Any kid button can get mad and go to fighting his head. You grew to manhood an hour ago, and a man don't fight like a boy."

"I'm listening," Dawson said, and he was strangely subdued.

"You and me are going to take old Jim into Vaca town," Cummings announced. "There might be those who will have things to say. Pay them no mind, Jeff. They might be playing into our hands!"

"It's going to be a chore if Terry Boyd gives me any slack-jaw," Jeff muttered. "But I'll give 'er a try, Gospel. I swear I'll try to keep down my mad."

"Spoken like a man, Jeff," Cummings praised. "That's the way old Jim would want it, and it's one of the last things we can do for that old cow-

34

feller. Now let's saddle the horses and use the night for travel. Safer that way, and if you find yourself called on to burn powder, just remember that it don't call for a killing!"

"I dunno," Jeff muttered. "I hate them 3 B fellers like I do a pack of side-winders. If they throw down on me, I don't know if I can throw off my shots the way you do!"

"You can try," Cummings answered. "And when a man tries hard, it's surprising the things he can do."

"I dunno," Jeff growled. "I tried to kill Terry Boyd, and I didn't quite make it. Mebbe I'm glad, but I ain't quite sure!"

Cummings changed the subject. "Give me a hand with old Jim. I'll lead his horse, and you can bring up the drag!"

CHAPTER THREE

Vaca town was just stirring to life when three horses came into town from the west, walking slowly up the wide dusty street. Gospel Cummings rode to the left, with Jeff Dawson on the right, and Jim Dawson's steel-dust was wedged in the middle with the body of his master roped to the old saddle.

A tall man dressed in funeral black stared at the three horses, and walked out to the rack in front of his store. There was no mistaking Boot Hill

Crandall, the local undertaker. Crandall ran a furniture store out in front; the rear of the long adobe building housed his funeral parlors. He spoke in a rich, mournful voice as the riders came abreast.

"Light down and rest your saddles, gents. Bring the late departed around the back way, that he may rest after his long ride!"

Gospel Cummings appeared annoyed, but Crandall was the only undertaker in Vaca. Jeff Dawson glared at Crandall, but he followed Cummings' example and dismounted.

"I will notify the coroner and the law," Crandall said with a slow smile. "A part of my regular service, at no extra cost."

"I can pay the cost," Dawson said icily. "I want the best coffin in the place, and Gospel will attend to the graveside services."

"That will be ten dollars more," Crandall said slowly.

"There will be no fee," Cummings said gently. "Jim Dawson was my friend, and an old saddlemate."

"Your business, of course," Crandall agreed. "My own business is cash at the graveside!"

"Which you'll get," Cummings said with a look of disapproval.

"This way, gentlemen," Crandall said, as Cummings threw off the ties that held the body to Jim Dawson's faithful horse. You brought a suit of his dress clothes?"

"Some shall be procured," Cummings answered shortly. "Jeff and I will buy them ourselves."

Crandall preceded the two men, and opened the back door. They carried the body of Jim Dawson into the preparation room, and Jeff hurried back to the horses. Cummings faced Crandall with a grim look on his bearded face.

"That gray casket, and how much?" he asked.

"I will present a detailed bill to Jeff Dawson," Crandall hedged.

Gospel Cummings spoke sternly. "The price is two hundred, and not a cent more," he said bluntly.

"Three hundred and twenty," Crandall argued.

"Look," Cummings answered. "They shot men like Billy the Kid and Jesse James. At least those two carried pistols when they held up a man!"

"I'll run my own business; you run yours," Crandall retorted.

"You run yours properly, or I'll ruin it," Cummings warned. "If I spread the word around town about what you are trying to do, some of the boys might drag you on the end of a rope, and it fastened to a running horse. Well?"

"Two hundred, cash at the graveside," Crandall muttered. "What you do is your own business, but I'm not in this business for my health."

"A man would never know it to look at you," Cummings said dryly. As you say, you are not in business for your health, but I notice you take mighty good care of it."

"Which it might pay you to do," Crandall retorted. "When the Boyds find out you took to siding the Lobo's whelp, they ain't going to like it none!"

"Let's get this straight," Cummings said slowly. "Jeff Dawson is not wanted by the law. I'd advise you not to let him hear you calling either him or old Jim out of their names."

"I was talking about the Boyds," Crandall hedged again. "I'll get about my duties, if it is all the same to you!"

Cummings nodded and went out to join Dawson, who was sitting his saddle impatiently. Cummings climbed his horse just as John Saint John came down the street at a fast walk. The big deputy had one hand on his belt-gun, but he loosened his grip when he saw Gospel.

"You're under arrest, Dawson!" the deputy barked.

"Just back up and start all over, Saint," Cummings said curtly. "What's the charge against Jeff?"

"Don't you interfere with me and my work," Saint John warned. "There might be charges placed against you for obstructing justice!"

"Fiddle-faddle," Cummings murmured scornfully. "Most times you are asking some of us to help you with your law chores."

"Which I'm not asking for any now," the big deputy barked. "This jasper is my prisoner, and I'm taking him down to the jail!"

"Uh, uh," Cummings interrupted again. "You ain't doing no such a thing."

"Are you telling me I can't arrest a criminal?" Saint John asked in a hoarse whisper.

"You go right ahead and arrest all the criminals you can find," Cummings answered evenly. "Now what's the charge against Jeff Dawson?"

"Rustling, attempted murder, and resisting arrest," Saint John blustered.

"One at a time," Cummings suggested, and he nodded when a dapper little man walked slowly forward to listen. "Howdy, Ace," he said. "I'd take it kindly if you'd listen in. You was saying, Saint?"

"The Boyd brothers claim this yearling is rustling 3 B beef," Saint John blustered.

"Did they sign a complaint?" Cummings asked. "Have they any proof?"

"Skip that for now," the deputy hedged. "Terry Boyd said he is almost sure the kid shot him."

"Tell Boyd he will have to be sure," Ace Fleming interrupted. "Now what's all this talk about Jeff resisting arrest?"

"I caught up with him down at Three Points," Saint John explained wrathfully. "I had him under my gun, when some pard of his snuck up behind and buffaloed me over the skull with the barrel of his gun!"

"You saw this attacker?" Fleming asked.

Saint John rubbed his head. "I saw stars, is all,"

39

he admitted. "When I roused around, the prisoner was gone!"

"Lucky for you he was," the gambler said. "You had no warrant for him, and he could have sued you and the County for false arrest!"

"Just a minute!" the deputy bellowed, and he turned to Dawson. "You saw this jigger who hit me. I demand to know his name!"

"It could have been Terry Boyd," Jeff answered spitefully.

"It wasn't Boyd," Saint John growled. "He'd have killed you just like he did for your Pa!"

Jeff Dawson clasped both hands on the horn of his saddle. The knuckles showed white, but Gospel Cummings interrupted before Dawson could answer.

"You're a disgrace to the badge you're wearing today, Saint," Cummings accused him. "Jim Dawson was Jeff's only kin, and we just brought the body in. If you was any kind of peace officer, you'd arrest Terry Boyd for murder!"

"Look, Gospel," Saint John said wrathfully. "You keep out of this, or I'll take it personal."

"So take it personal," Gospel Cummings answered. "Take it any way you want it, and start any time you think you're ready."

His bearded face was hard as Cummings stared at the big deputy. Saint John blew through his lips for lack of something to say. Finally he found his voice.

"Jim Dawson was wanted, and there was a price on his scalp," the deputy retorted. "Terry Boyd will get that thousand dollars, and like you know, it's always open season on lobos!"

"Big feller," Jeff Dawson said quietly, "some day I'm going to make you eat your words. Jim Dawson was an honest man, which is more than I can say for those who framed him!"

No one interrupted. Saint John cleared his throat, and appeared embarrassed. "I'm the law here," he blustered finally. "Are you threatening the law?"

"Uh, uh," Dawson murmured. "Just making a promise."

"You want to make something out of that?" Gospel Cummings asked angrily.

"What's it to you?" the deputy demanded.

"Jim Dawson and me rode the range together down in Texas," Cummings answered, and his tone was brittle. "Jim was honest in everything he ever did. He was my saddle-pard, and I'm siding his chip. You can pass that word to the Boyds if you're so minded. Come on, Jeff; we've got some shopping to do!"

Ace Fleming owned the casino, though he seldom ran the games since he had married Sandra Carson. Fleming also owned the prosperous Circle F cattle spread. He stood about five-feet-five in his polished boots, but Fleming was one of the strongest men in Vaca. Now

41

Fleming glanced at Cummings, and then turned his full gaze upon the big deputy sheriff. He frowned when he noted the stubborn tilt to Saint John's rugged jaw, and the gambler's voice held a challenge as he addressed Saint John.

"I've known you for a long time, Saint," he told the deputy. "Are you rodding the law here, or are you taking sides with the Boyds?"

"I'm rodding the law!" Saint John answered hotly.

"Then you rod it legal," Fleming suggested, and he walked back to the casino.

Gospel Cummings and Jeff Dawson went to the general store and bought a complete outfit of clothing for the dead man. A tall old cattleman waited at the tie-rail in front of the store. He stepped up and offered his right hand to Dawson.

"Glad to see you again, Jeff," he said heartily. "You need any help that Gospel can't give you, call on Cole Brighton!"

Jeff Dawson swallowed hard and nodded his head. "Thanks, Cole," he murmured huskily. He glanced up the street and suddenly stiffened. Cummings followed the cowboy's glance, and loosened the heavy six-shooter on his right leg.

"Steady, boy," he warned Dawson. "They won't get far if they make trouble!"

The Boyd brothers rode up to the store and dismounted from their 3 B horses. Tom Boyd was the oldest; a man of perhaps forty. He was tall, lathy thin, and his pale blue eyes were cold and slitted as he stared at Jeff Dawson. Dixon Boyd was five years younger than his brother, but cut on the same general pattern. Both had the lazy grace of the born saddle athlete, but Dawson knew that the laziness was deceptive.

Dixon Boyd spoke to Gospel Cummings from the side of his mouth, and his eyes never left the face of young Dawson.

"This is between us and that outlaw's cub, Cummings. We're taking him for the law or killing him, one!"

"Hold it!" Cummings warned sternly. "The law has already talked to Jeff. There's no charge agin him; no warrant out for his arrest!"

"I'll take Dixon, Gospel!" Jeff Dawson said eagerly. "You watch that other side-winder. They brought it to me!"

"You stay out of this, Cummings!" Tom Boyd warned. "Was a time when outlaws were shot on sight, but this country is going soft!"

"They was shot on sight up to yesterday," Jeff Dawson said grimly. "She's some different when you gents have to face a victim with an even break. How's your brother Terry, the sneakin' son?"

Tom Boyd set his jaw and glanced at his brother. "Say when," he whispered. "I believe this whelp shot Terry!"

"You take Dixon, Gospel," Jeff Dawson said again. "That way all hands will know their targets!"

"You want it that way?" Cummings asked Tom Boyd slowly.

"It ain't none of your put in," Tom Boyd hedged.

"I've bought chips in this game," Gospel Cummings announced. "And Ace Fleming has a stack to play in any game you deal!"

"I'll put in my ante," old Cole Brighton added.

"Think it over, boys," Cummings suggested. "You Boyd fellers can't just ride down and shoot a yearling to make you a reputation."

"Mebbe this ain't the time or place," Tom Boyd said slowly. "It's a good thing this lobo's whelp came in out of the tangles."

"That's right," Cummings agreed. "Back there a feller can sneak up and shoot a man before he knows he's in danger. If that same thing happens in town, the law will call it murder!"

John Saint John walked up and listened intently. He plucked at his long cowhorn mustaches, and Tom Boyd turned to the deputy.

"Is Gospel telling it straight?" he demanded. "He says this Dawson maverick ain't wanted any more!"

"He's telling it straight," Saint John answered curtly. "And after this, I'll thank you 3 B hombres to let the law do the work it gets paid to do."

"Rustling is anybody's business," Dixon Boyd

said nastily. "If we catch a rustler on our range, we won't need any help from the law."

"That works two ways," Jeff Dawson spoke up quietly. "If I catch any killers or thieves on the Triangle D, I likewise won't need any help from the law!"

Tom Boyd appeared startled. "Meaning you are going back to the run-down Triangle D?" he asked.

"He owns every foot of it," Gospel Cummings interrupted. "Ace Fleming paid the taxes, and kept Jeff's foundation herd under the Triangle D iron. Jeff is a friend of mine, like old Jim was before him. I wouldn't want to hear about anything funny happening to Jeff!"

"He gets trigger-happy, us Boyds will know what to do," Tom Boyd said nastily. "We ride across that Triangle D range upon occasion to round up our strays!"

"And I might ride across 3 B graze to look for my own stock," Jeff Dawson said quietly. "Fair enough with you fellers?"

"You stay off 3 B range! "Dixon Boyd interrupted harshly.

"So you dealt the cards, and I'll play them that way," Dawson said coldly. "I got no time for a rule that don't measure the same distance from the middle to either end. You can tell Terry I said so. And tell him I mean to square up for what he did to old Jim!"

"Tell him likewise that I'm siding Jeff." Cummings had his say. "Any play he makes from now on had better be cut in the clear!"

"Slow down on that war talk!" Saint John warned. "All you hombres are right here in Vaca town. If I can't do anything else, I can wrap the calabozo around the lot of you for disturbing the peace!"

"You heard the law," Cummings said gently, "I'm for settling all differences peacefully."

"I'll give you five dollars an acre for those two sections," Tom Boyd told Dawson. "It ain't worth more than two."

"Better buy some other land for two," Jeff Dawson said coldly. "The Triangle D ain't for sale."

Dixon Boyd looked over Jeff Dawson's saddle with impudent inquiry. "Glad to see you don't pack a running iron," he sneered.

"Don't judge other people by yourself!" Jeff Dawson said hotly. "A dog that will fetch a bone will carry one!"

"You accusing me of rustling?" Dixon Boyd demanded.

"Right back at you, cow-feller," Dawson countered. "Are you accusing me of the same?"

"Pass it for now," Dixon murmured. "But if I catch you . . ."

Dixon Boyd mounted his horse and jerked his head at his brother. Jeff Dawson stood wide-legged, staring at them as long as they were in sight: Gospel Cummings spoke quietly.

"Better stay with me for a few days, Jeff. Then I'll ride out to the Triangle D with you, and help you get started again. Now I got a few little things to do; I'll meet you here in an hour."

"Thanks for everything, Gospel," Dawson said gratefully. "I'd have been in a tight if you hadn't spoke up, and I wasn't expecting much of a shake from the law!"

"You'll get a fair shake, yearling," Saint John said sourly. "But don't go throwing your weight around too much, because you don't weigh enough just yet!"

"I'll take care of myself, and you do the same," Dawson answered the scowling lawman. "I'll see you in an hour, Gospel."

Cummings mounted his sorrel and rode up the street. He turned at the corner, rode to an alley, and turned in. A moment later he knocked at the back door of the casino.

The bartender came to the door, a fat man with a lock of greasy black hair curled over his left eye.

"Step in and have one on the house, Gospel," the bartender invited.

"You're a comical cuss, Fat Farrell," Cummings said dryly. "I never drink on the premises, like you know. Wrap me up four quarts of Three Daisies in a fairly recent newspaper."

"You mean you've learned to read?" Fat Farrell asked with a straight face.

"Yeah," Cummings answered with a smile. "I

learned to read back in Texas where they use up smart bardogs fast. Them that didn't learn to read all turned out to be bartenders, and most of them were fat!"

"So they was men of sterling courage," Farrell said with a shrug. "Being too fat to run fast, they had to learn to fight!"

Cummings recognized something significant in Farrell's words. The two were fast friends. "What is it, Fat?" he asked in a low whisper.

Fat Farrell stepped closer and spoke in a whisper. "Tom Boyd was talking some, Gospel," he growled. "He allowed that as soon as his brother Terry got over his headache, he'd be looking for young Jeff Dawson. Thought you ought to know, seeing that you are riding herd on that yearling for a spell."

"Thanks, bardog," Cummings said gratefully. "Forewarned is forearmed."

Farrell disappeared and returned a moment later with the bottles wrapped in a newspaper. Cummings took the package, mounted his horse, waved a friendly hand at Farrell, and rode down the alley. Cummings reined his horse to a stop when he saw Jeff Dawson facing two cowboys in front of the long saloon.

Both were youngsters, not much older than Jeff. One was a tall lean waddy with a shock of red hair. His partner was shorter, with wide powerful shoulders, and they had Jeff Dawson between them. The redhead was speaking.

"Better fork your bronc and quit the country, you owl-hooter. We catch you in town after twelve o'clock, we aim to make you hard to find!"

Dawson watched the two 3 B punchers, and he knew he was caught in a cross-fire if gun-play began. Then he saw Cummings drop from his horse at the far end of the tie-rail.

"Don't crowd me, Red," Dawson warned the taller cowboy. "Or did you have to get Shorty to back up your wau-wau?"

"Outlaws is like side-winders." Shorty spoke raspingly. "The little ones is as dangerous as the big ones. You heard Red give you time enough to clear out, and you better fan your bronc op the hind legs going away!"

"Empty barrels make the most noise." Dawson sneered.

"Twelve o'clock is deadline for rustlers," Red Stang said in a low lazy drawl.

Without warning, Dawson stepped forward like a cat, jabbed the tall redhead with a stiff left, and crossed his right fist to the jaw. As his pard went down, the blocky 3 B puncher leaped at Dawson.

Gospel Cummings stepped forward and swung his flat hand hard against Shorty's head. "Stay out of it, Shorty," Cummings growled. "You ain't running in a wolf-pack now!"

Red Stang rolled up and rushed at Jeff Dawson. Jeff avoided the savage charge, and clipped Stang behind the ear as the lanky cowboy rushed past.

Then Dawson followed him, pouring hard rights and lefts to the bony face of his taller opponent.

Red Stang stood up under the punishment, trying to catch hold with his long powerful arms. Gospel Cummings leaned against the tie-rail to watch, a little smile curling his bearded lips.

Jeff Dawson allowed a long arm to slide over his shoulder. As Red Stang tightened that arm, Dawson turned swiftly, caught the thick wrist, and bucked down as he pulled at the same time. It was the flying mare; the same hold Cummings had used on Dawson back in the cave near Lost River.

Red Stang flew through the air and landed hard on his back and shoulders. Dawson was after him fast. As Stang came to his feet, Jeff Dawson drove in with all his weight behind a straight right which caught Red Stang flush on the point of his bony jaw.

Stang stiffened, his boots left the ground, and then the lanky redhead fell face forward in the trampled dust. Jeff Dawson turned to Shorty Benson.

"I never did get enough fight," he said crisply. "You're next, you barn-shouldered coyote!"

"This time you'll get enough fight," Shorty Benson growled savagely. "The 3 B don't like rustlers, and we fight for the iron that pays us our wages!"

"So if that 3 B outfit is rustlers, what does that make you?" Dawson asked with a hard smile.

showing his white teeth. "Bring it to me, you hoop-legged pelican!"

Shorty Benson made a savage rush and sat down hard when a rocky fist exploded under his jaw. He shook his head, but refused to get to his feet.

"I don't fight much with my hands," he said coldly. "You want to make it with smoke-poles?"

"Suits me," Dawson agreed.

John Saint John stepped out of his office and shouted. His law-gun was in his big right hand.

"You, Shorty Benson. You and Red Stang climb your saddles and get on out of town. I saw this whole go-around!"

The 3 B cowboys mounted their horses and rode toward the east. Red Stang had had enough fight, but Shorty Benson growled threats as he passed Gospel Cummings.

"I'll square for that belt you hung on me, old-timer. I'll catch you when you don't have the law to back up your tin-horn play!"

"Whoa, Shorty," Cummings said softly. "Mebbe you better settle with me now so's we can keep you honest. I don't like the look in your squinchy eyes, and I'd hate to have you sneak up behind me when I wasn't looking!"

"Drift!" Saint John shouted at Benson. "Or I'll lodge you in jail for disturbing the peace!"

Shorty Benson started his horse. "You heard me, you Holy Joe!" he growled at Cummings. "I'll square with you!"

Gospel Cummings made no answer. He mounted his horse, thanked Saint John with a nod of his head, and waited for Dawson to mount his Morgan.

"Let's get out to Three Points," he suggested. "We didn't get any sleep last night."

CHAPTER FOUR

Red Stang rubbed the swelling on his jaw as he dismounted at the rail in front of the 3 B bunkhouse. Shorty Benson was scowling and muttering to himself. He faced Red, touched the handle of his six-shooter, and spoke jerkily.

"You can report to the bosses, Red. I want to clean my gun. A hand never knows when he might stumble over a snake again!"

"Meaning Gospel Cummings?" Stang asked curiously.

Benson nodded.

Red Stang shrugged. "It's your business, but you've taken on quite a chore," he remarked carelessly. "Cummings is just about the fastest and best shot in these parts, and he's plenty seasoned!"

"So he's seasoned long enough!" Benson grunted. "You can let me know what Tom Boyd has to say."

Stang nodded and tied up his horse. He high-heeled it across the big yard to the ranch house where the three Boyd brothers lived together. Tom Boyd looked up from an old scarred oaken desk as Red Stang entered the big front room.

"You run into a door?" he asked the tall redhead.

"I ran into the hardest bunch of knuckles so far up to now," Stang answered honestly. "Is it going to be open war between the 3 B and the Triangle D?" he asked.

Terry Boyd was lying on a cowskin couch, with a bandage covering his head. He sat up when Stang mentioned the Triangle D.

"What about that shoe-string outfit?" Terry Boyd demanded.

"Me and Shorty Benson just come back from town," Stang reported. "We saw Jeff Dawson and his pards."

"You mean Gospel Cummings?" Tom Boyd asked.

Stang nodded. "Him and Ace Fleming," he answered. "Me and Shorty gave Dawson until twelve o'clock to leave town. But we didn't make it stick," he admitted.

"Who told you to horn in on a closed play?" Tom demanded angrily.

"Hold it, Tom," Terry interrupted. "Let's hear the rest of it. It ought to be good, judging from the lump on Red's jaw!"

Stang scowled and glanced at the bandage on Terry Boyd's black head. "I'm thankful it wasn't a slug that hit me," he said nastily.

"Why, you salty splinter!" Terry Boyd shouted, and leaped to his feet.

"Sit down, Terry!" Tom Boyd said sternly. "We

might need all the help we can get if Ace Fleming is in this thing now!"

"I don't aim to take slack from the riding hands," Terry snarled.

"You can't be any tougher than Jeff Dawson," Stang retorted. "What's holding you back?"

"A head wound, that's, what!" Tom Boyd spoke up swiftly. "Get on with your story, Red!"

"I tied into Dawson with my maulies," Stang confessed. "He whipped me from here to who hid the broom, but he didn't stomp me none with his boots!"

"Yeah, and where was Shorty all this time?" Tom Boyd asked sarcastically. "I thought Shorty was rough, tough, and nasty."

"Gospel Cummings rode up," Stang explained. "He told Shorty to stay out of it, and he slapped Shorty a backhander when Benson paid him no mind!"

Terry Boyd sneered. "What do you two nannies carry hog-legs for, may I ask?"

"You can have Cummings," Stang answered slowly. "I don't hanker to match my fair-to-middlin' draw agin that old Injun fighter!"

"Leastwise you're honest, Red," Tom Boyd commented. "But I'm surprised that Benson took it laying down!"

"He asked for gun-fight," Stang said slowly. "But the law stepped in and threatened to wrap the jail around us. Shorty swears he will even the tally with Cummings!"

"Might be we can use Shorty," Terry Boyd murmured thoughtfully.

"You might as well get back to the bunkhouse," Tom Boyd said quickly to Stang.

"Like you said, Boss," Stang answered, and left the room.

Terry Boyd glared at his older brother, but Tom did not look at him. He seemed lost in thought. "Sometimes I ain't so sure," he muttered.

"I am!" Terry spoke up. "That yearling has to go!"

Tom Boyd turned and looked at his brother. "Look, Terry," he said forcefully. "I meant I am not sure that Jim Dawson stole our payroll that time."

"He stole it," Terry growled. "And I paid him off for it!"

"I didn't see the play," Tom answered. "Young Jeff claims you shot his old man on a sneak!"

"Just a minute, Tom," Terry argued. "Now say a rattlesnake was getting set to fang you. What would you do?"

"Well, I'd know it if he was," Tom Boyd answered promptly. "He'd rattle a warning unless he was a side-winder!"

"So now I'm a side-winder," Terry Boyd muttered.

"Don't bait me, Terry!" Tom shouted. "You was talking about a rattler getting set to fang me. With all his faults, Jim Dawson would give a man warning every time!"

"Answer my question!" Terry insisted. "Am I a side-winder?"

"You answer mine first," Tom came back at his angry brother. "Did you shoot old Jim Dawson without warning?"

"I beat him to the draw," Terry shouted.

"So call yourself names if you want to argue," Tom Boyd snapped. "I offered Dawson five dollars an acre for those two sections which make up his Triangle D range, and he turned me down."

"He ain't grazing his stock on it yet," Terry answered. "We could ride over there and look around before he makes up his mind."

"That's another thing," Tom argued stubbornly. "I never have been sure that treasure was brought up here, and if it was, it's stolen loot."

"Well, I ain't particular," Terry grunted. "Dirty money gets clean when it changes hands twice!"

"Me and Dixon has stayed right here running the 3 B spread," Tom said wrathfully, "while you took off every so often and choused around all over the country!"

"So I took a little vacation every once in a while," Terry Boyd answered. "I wanted to learn what other cattlemen were doing to improve their herds, and besides, I needed the change!"

"And you lost more money gambling than both me and Dix made," Tom Boyd growled. "Like you know, you don't own a one-third interest in the 3 B any more!"

"That's where you're wrong," Terry corrected. "I owe you and Dix a few thousand dollars. When I pay that back, I still own a third in this outfit."

"So that's why you are so interested in finding that outlaw loot," Torn said thinly. "If we find it, we'd turn it over to the rightful owners, and take our share of the rewards!"

"That would depend on who found it first," Terry Boyd said plainly. "What about that funeral tomorrow?"

"What about it?" Tom Boyd asked.

"I'm going," Terry announced. "I tallied for that old outlaw, and I'll get a lot of pleasure in attending the planting!"

Tom Boyd changed the subject. "There's good water on the Triangle D that we could use. I'd like to have that spring to save moving our stock to summer range."

"We can buy it after I find that treasure," Terry Boyd said lazily. "You going to the planting tomorrow?"

Tom Boyd slammed his feet to the floor and stomped from the room without speaking. He was known as a hard man at a bargain, but he also had the reputation of being honest. He met his brother Dixon just riding into the big yard, and Dixon swung down from the saddle.

"What put you on the prod again, Tom?" Dixon asked. "As if I didn't know," he added. "You've been sitting up with the patient."

"Look, Dix," Tom asked suddenly. "Where do you stand on this outlaw treasure old Fred Haney was babbling about?"

"Finders keepers with me," Dixon answered slowly. "We're in the hole pretty deep on account of Terry gambling the way he did."

"But if it was on the Triangle D?" Tom persisted.

Dixon Boyd rubbed his stubbled jaw. "As a matter of law, it would belong to the owner of the land," he answered. "That is, if the finder kept his mouth shut about it."

"So the Triangle D belongs to young Dawson," Tom clinched his point. "You heard what he said about trespassers."

"Yeah, but Terry didn't hear him," Dixon said with a smile. "Terry means to get that money, and we could use some right now!"

"I don't want that kind of money," Tom Boyd said grimly.

"I reckon you're right, Tom," Dixon agreed. "But the rewards for finding that treasure would put us in the clear, and I'd settle for that!"

"Another thing," Tom Boyd continued. "Do you still think that old Jim Dawson stole our 3 B payroll that time?"

"Everything points that way, Tom. Jim Dawson was trying to get a start on that run-down little Triangle D, and he needed money bad. There wasn't any outlaws in the neighbourhood after old

Fred Haney died, and the tracks led right to the Triangle D!"

"Gospel Cummings is siding the Lobo's whelp now," Tom Boyd said, and he watched his brother closely.

"I heard about it," Dixon answered. "Gospel Cummings is a hard man to fool. He can ride sign where another man wouldn't see any, and he's a square-shooter."

"And he was saddle-pard to Jim Dawson down in Texas when they were yearlings," Tom added. "We'll have to go easy there, Dix."

"Those two sections making up the Triangle D graze," Dixon said slowly. "Mebbe Jeff Dawson would sell if we offered him a fair price. We need that flowing spring, and we just might find that outlaw loot. Offer him ten dollars an acre the next time, and if that don't work, like as not we can scare him out in time."

"His old man didn't scare easy," Tom reminded him. "It took a killing to get shut of that old rawhide!"

"We should have signed a complaint with Saint John," Dixon complained. "Terry said he had proof that some 3 B beef had been rustled."

"All I saw was one steer hide where Jim Dawson had killed one of our critters for camp-meat," Tom said thoughtfully. "We've killed a beef many's the time when we were getting us a start."

"Terry's out to get Jeff Dawson," Dixon said.

"You reckon he beefed old Jim on a sneak?"

"Well, he's brother to you and me," Tom drawled. "Terry claims he beat that old owl-hooter to the draw!"

"Yeah, he's our brother," Dixon answered gruffly. "But he ain't much like you and me, Tom."

Red Stang entered the long 3 B bunkhouse and sprawled on his bunk. Shorty Benson was cleaning his six-shooter. He looked up and glared at the tall redhead.

"What did the old man say?" he demanded. "About the way that old sin-buster tied into us?"

"He didn't say," Stang answered. "Except that he wanted to know who told us to horn in on a closed play."

"The next one will be on me," Benson promised grimly. "I don't take it too hard if some other hard-case beats me to the draw, but the man don't live and keep on living who can belt me with the flat of his hand!"

"There was some talk up there about rattlesnakes," Stang told Benson. "Old Tom allowed that a diamond-back always rattled a warning, while a side-winder was apt to sneak up on a man and strike without warning. Him and Terry had quite an argument about it, on account of the way old Jim Dawson was killed."

"I'll string along with Terry," Benson stated promptly.

"I see you've got your hog-leg cleaned up good," Stang said, as he glanced at Benson's six-shooter.

"Yeah; I'm all set for some snake-killin' on my own," Benson boasted coldly.

"Side-winder or diamond-back?" Stang asked quietly.

Shorty Benson dropped his hand down to his holstered gun. "I don't like yore attitude, feller," he said savagely.

Red Stang sat up and dropped his boots to the floor. Then he stood up swiftly, facing Shorty Benson.

"I don't like yours any better," he snapped. "Well?"

Shorty Benson dropped his hand away from his holster. "We ought to do our fighting together," he suggested slowly.

Red Stang smiled grimly as he relaxed. "You got a poor memory, Shorty," he reminded Benson. "We did some fighting together not so long ago, and we came out second best!"

"That's because what passes for the law in these parts horned in," Benson growled.

"Yeah, him and Gospel Cummings," Stang agreed.

"So you take Dawson and leave Cummings to me," Benson suggested. "I can handle my end."

Red Stang shook his head. "I'm just a riding hand on the 3 B. Dawson whipped me fair and square. I'll give him that much."

"His old man was an owl-hooter!" Benson declared viciously. "In my tally book, that chip of his is the same thing!"

Red Stang seemed to change at the mention of outlaws. He sat down on his bunk and leaned forward. His voice was low and brittle when he spoke.

"Some times there ain't much difference between an outlaw and a lot of other fellers who never did get caught," he told Shorty Benson. "Sometimes a feller gets framed for something he never did, and then he can't quit the gang!"

"Gwan!" Benson scoffed. "You talk like you might have straddled the owl-hoot trail yourself one time!"

"And if I did?" Stang asked softly.

Shorty Benson looked up and stared at Stang. "That's your own business," he conceded swiftly. "And that reminds me, Red. What do you think about all this talk about outlaw loot being hid out somewhere in these parts?"

Now the anger had left Red Stang, and he shook his head listlessly. "No matter where you go, there's always a lot of talk about buried treasure," he answered carelessly. "What if there was some, and we found it?" he asked. "It would belong to the bosses, and we wouldn't even get a cut of the rewards!"

"We would, if we found it first," Benson said slyly. "The talk is that it is in money, and a lot of jewels. A couple of smart hombres could hide the stuff until they were ready to draw their time and ride on out to see what was on the other side of the hill."

"That's what I mean," Stang said bluntly. "The outlaws are the ones who get caught."

He stopped talking and turned to face the door. Tom Boyd walked in and glared at the two cowboys.

"Did the cooky ring the triangle for supper?" Boyd asked bluntly.

"I didn't hear it," Benson answered, and then he glanced at Boyd's face. "It was too late to ride out to the crew," he excused his loafing.

"So you and Red better get out to the corrals and rack up some hay for the saddle-stock," Tom Boyd suggested.

"Like you said," Stang answered, and started for the door.

Shorty Benson got up slowly and asked a question, "Are we going to the burying tomorrow, Boss?"

Tom Boyd frowned for a moment. "Was the deceased kin of yours?" he asked Benson.

"You know he wasn't," Benson growled. "Just thought you might want the crew to ride along to back up any play you might make!"

"At a burying?" Tom Boyd asked sharply.

"Just thought I'd ask," Benson muttered, and started for the door.

"Just a minute, Shorty," Tom Boyd said sternly. "If I was you, I'd forget about taking smoke to Gospel Cummings. You couldn't beat him with a square shake, and we don't want any of the other kind. Do you get my meaning?"

"I get you, Boss," Benson answered gruffly, and he hurried from the bunkhouse to hide the anger which smouldered in his gray eyes.

As Tom Boyd left the bunkhouse, he was met by Terry who had removed the bandage from his head.

"Might be a good idea to have the boys ride over to the planting tomorrow," Terry Boyd suggested. "I don't mean to start any trouble," he added quickly, when his brother frowned. "Just to show the folks we stick together, and that we don't bluff easy."

"We'll go, but don't you start anything, Terry," Tom Boyd warned his younger brother. "Dix and I don't play the way you do, and we mean to stay here in business!"

"Lay your hackles, Tom," Terry said soothingly. "After all, we did the law a favor, and I still don't trust Jeff Dawson none to speak of!"

"Then why speak of it?" Tom Boyd retorted. "When we get the goods on young Dawson, we'll ride in and sign a complaint. Saint John might not be too bright, but he's a tough man to buck in a law-fight!"

"Yeah, and he makes a big target," Terry said

carelessly. "He's made plenty of enemies in these parts."

"That goes for all of us, and don't you forget it, Terry. There are a lot of people in these parts who don't like you too well!"

"I'll take care of myself," Terry Boyd said coldly.

Tom and Terry started for the big house, where they were joined by Dixon. "We'll all ride over to the burying tomorrow," Terry announced, and he watched Dixon's weathered face. "We won't make any trouble, but all the neighbors will be there, and we can't very well do any less."

"Well, cut my cinchas," Dixon Boyd murmured. "Mebbe that bullet slap Terry got on the head did him some good, Tom," he remarked to his older brother. "What he says makes sense."

"That little burn on the skull had nothing to do with it," Terry denied angrily. "It's just that it will cause a lot of talk if we don't go. And like I was telling Tom a while ago, it will make a show of strength where it will do the most good!"

"Yeah, that's right," Dixon agreed. "Cole Brighton and his crew will be there, as well as Ace Fleming and the Circle F crowd, Singin' Saunders and the Wagonner outfit, to mention a few."

Terry Boyd scowled. He knew that Dixon was reading off the solid respectable cattlemen in the Strip, and the implication was not lost on Terry.

"We're as big as any one of those outfits by

themselves," Terry said smoothly. "There ain't an outfit in these parts that has any time for rustlers!"

"So we will find the rustlers first, if any," Tom Boyd said with finality. "If you start a personal ruckus, Terry, just bear in mind it will be personal!"

"I'll keep it in mind," Terry growled. "But I've got my suspicions, and I mean to make them something more. I still own a slice of this outfit, and I mean to protect my own interests!"

"That's a good idea, and gives me something to think about," Tom Boyd said quietly. "Me and Dix would be better off right now if we'd protected our interests a little better."

"So that bullet-crease Terry got did us all some good," Dixon added with a grin, in an attempt to ease the tension.

Terry Boyd scowled as he gingerly felt his head. "I won't forget about that bullet-crease," he promised and, whirling on his high heel, he walked rapidly to the big barn.

CHAPTER FIVE

Gospel Cummings was glad to see the large crowd which had gathered to pay their last respects to Jim Dawson. Circumstantial evidence had been strong against old Jim, but most of the cattlemen had believed in his innocence.

Gospel took his place at the head of the grave;

Jeff Dawson faced him from the foot, his face composed but pale. He and Jim had been closer than most fathers and sons, especially since they had been hiding out from the law in the badlands. His jaw tightened as he vowed again to clear his father's name.

The mourners gathered around, reverently removing their hats. Gospel Cummings glanced at a little group of men some distance away. He spoke gently.

"All gentlemen will please remove their head-gear out of respect for the deceased!"

None of the men made a move to uncover their heads. They all stood close to horses wearing the 3 B brand. The Boyd brothers stood together, with Terry Boyd in the middle. All carried six-shooters in their holsters.

Shorty Benson stood near Terry Boyd, and Shorty leered at Gospel Cummings from under the lowered brim of his floppy Stetson. Red Stang was not in the group.

Gospel Cummings ignored Shorty Benson. He focused his attention on Terry Boyd, who glared back at him with open hostility plain on his thin, bony face. The cattlemen sensed the strange silent duel, and they watched intently.

"I shall speak but once more!" Gospel Cummings said firmly. "All gentlemen will please remove their hats!"

A deep brooding silence fell across the place of

the dead. None of the 3 B crowd made any move to obey the suggestion.

Gospel Cummings held his worn Bible in his left hand. His right hand whipped down and up with orange flame outlining the black muzzle of his six-shooter. The new gray Stetson leaped from the head of Terry Boyd like a thing alive.

As if motivated by a common impulse, every man in the 3 B crew quickly doffed his headgear. Terry Boyd snarled, "I didn't have any respect for the deceased!"

"Silence!" Cummings roared. "Another word from you and I will do more than just part your hair with a slug!"

Terry Boyd set his thin lips in a straight line, but he kept his hand carefully away from his holstered six-shooter.

"So it was you who bushed me from the brush," he whispered.

"If I had shot you, you would not have the use of your gun-hand today," Cummings answered stiffly. "Now we will proceed with the services. All other matters can wait."

Gospel Cummings holstered his smoking pistol and composed his features. He read from the Book, and his deep voice was rich and musical. Then he closed the book and glanced around at the faees of the mourners.

"Jim Dawson was my friend, and an honest man," Cummings began his eulogy. "His life was

an open book for all to read. He was a good hus-
band, a devoted father, and a tophand cowboy. He
was forced into flight by circumstances beyond
his control, but now he has found peace and rest at
last. His son has come back to us, a clean and
honest man. Jim Dawson was wrongfully accused,
but I want to say that the truth, though crushed to
earth, shall rise again. Murder will out, and the
killer lives with his conscience!"

He stopped to glance at Terry Boyd, but the
youngest of the brothers merely glared. Gospel
Cummings continued his eulogy.

"I knew Jim Dawson when he was no older than
his son Jeff. He was a cowboy down in Texas on
the old XIT spread. He had the respect of every
honest man in Texas, just as he had here in
Arizona. I was proud to call him friend!"

He leaned over and picked up a clod of earth.
Breaking it between his strong brown fingers,
Gospel Cummings said a solemn farewell to his
old saddle-pard. "*Vaya con Dios, amigo!*"

Jeff Dawson repeated clearly: "Go thou with
God, friend!"

Old Cole Brighton spoke solemnly, to echo the
thought. "Amen," he said reverently.

Several other old cattlemen echoed the last
farewell, and they watched the 3 B crowd with
hostile eyes. Most of them respected Tom Boyd,
but few of them had any liking for Terry Boyd,
who was a known wastrel.

Gospel Cummings lowered his head and closed his eyes. He said a brief but eloquent prayer, calling on the Big Ramrod up yonder to lead Jim Dawson into the Green Pastures. After concluding the services, Cummings walked slowly from the grave, made his way between the headstones, and entered his cabin. He heard the glass hearse rattle through the portals of the graveyard, and roll back to town. Then the thud of many hooves, and after a time, the sound of young voices near the tie-rail at one side of the cabin.

A smile lighted his face as Cummings glanced out and saw Jeff Dawson talking to a pretty girl. The two young people were conscious only of each other, and Jeff was holding the girl's left hand.

"I've missed you something wonderful, Connie," he said, and his voice sounded strained. "Three years is a long time."

Connie Brighton smiled and nodded her head. "I missed you, too, Jeff," she whispered. "You'll come to see me sometimes?"

"Come to the ranch to see you?" Jeff Dawson asked in a wondering tone. "You're asking the Lobo's whelp to come into your house?"

"I'm asking Jim Dawson's son to come and see me and my folks," Connie corrected him gravely. "Jim was a good cowman, and honest. Father has always believed in Jim, and I know his son is honest and fine!"

"Gee!" Jeff whispered. "Dad always said things would clear up, but three years is a mighty long time to wait!"

"So you have three years to make up," Connie said with a smile. "You've grown a lot, Jeff, and you seem so much more mature!"

"That's what old Gospel said," Jeff murmured.

"Come soon, Jeff," Connie urged. "I want you to meet Mother so she can see how much you have changed for the better!"

"I'll come," Jeff promised.

"You will be careful, Jeff? I mean, about Terry Boyd," Connie added.

Jeff Dawson's boyish face hardened. "He killed Dad," he said thickly. "I don't know how much more I can take from those 3 B fellers!"

Gospel Cummings listened with a frown. He remembered the scene at the grave; the accusations of the Boyd brothers in Vaca town.

Connie surprised Cummings by saying, "A man can take only so much. But promise me one thing, Jeff."

"Yeah."

"Just don't start anything with them," the girl pleaded. "You've got lots of friends in town, and Gospel will help you."

Cummings nodded his head in agreement. His eyes widened when Connie Brighton put a protecting arm around the cowboy's shoulders.

"I'll help, too—all I can," she whispered.

Gospel Cummings had the grace to turn away when Dawson folded the girl in his strong young arms and kissed her tenderly. After a moment he heard Jeff say, "I'll ride back to town with you, Connie!"

"Perhaps you had better not leave Gospel alone here," Connie demurred. "After that little quarrel he had with the Boyds!"

"Don't you worry none about Gospel," Jeff told the girl. "He's the fastest hombre with a hand-gun I ever saw, and he can call his shots."

Cummings sighed as the young couple mounted their horses and rode towards Vaca. The tall plainsman changed to his old clothes, and then he sat down to clean his pistol. He frowned for a moment, arose quickly, took a spare forty-five from under his bunk, and seated it in his worn holster.

With the touch of gun metal in his hands, Gospel Cummings seemed to change. The gentleness left his face, and his eyes lost their brooding sorrow. After carefully cleaning every moving part, Cummings placed the weapon on the table and washed his hands in the granite basin. He was drying his hands when a man's voice spoke.

"Elevate, you Holy Joe! I've got you over a barrel!"

Gospel Cummings turned his head slowly. Shorty Benson stood framed in the open doorway with a cocked six-shooter in his grimy right fist.

"Slapped me open-handed yesterday morning, remember?" Benson sneered. "The man don't live who can do that to Shorty Benson!"

"I'm still living," Cummings said quietly.

"That's right, but I can fix it," Benson said grimly. "If you've got any little old prayers to say for yourself, start mumbling!"

"Give me a chance," Cummings pleaded. "My gun is on the table. Holster yours and give me a chance to break for my hardware!"

"Say! That ain't a bad idea," Benson answered. "I can let you get your smoke-pole in your fist, and cut you down before you can thumb back the trigger. That way, it will be self-defense!"

Gospel Cummings hesitated to gain time for some quick thinking. He had no illusions about Shorty Benson, or Shorty's version of fair play.

Gospel Cummings straightened slowly. Suddenly he remembered Jim Dawson's old gun which he had tried in his holster for size, and which was still snugged down in the worn leather.

"Did you finish yore prayers?" Benson asked mockingly.

"Just a minute, Shorty," Cummings said quickly. "I'm sorry I slapped you yesterday morning. You can slap me to even the score. This don't call for a killing!"

"It calls for a killing!" Benson said quickly. "I said I'd get you, and I always keep my word. Now I'm going to holster my cutter, and you start scrambling for that gun on the table whenever you're so minded!"

Gospel Cummings still had his back to the killer. The tails of his long coat hid the spare weapon he had placed in his holster, and his hands were free from oil. His next move was like the unexpected clap of heat lighting.

Cummings whirled on one boot-heel. His right hand slapped down just as Shorty Benson clawed for the gun in his open holster. Gospel Cummings' six-shooter snouted above the holster, and roared thunderously just as Benson's weapon was clearing leather.

The bullet struck Benson's hand, and his own gun exploded to send a slug into the floor at his feet. Benson was swung around, and he went to his knees under the shock of the heavy bullet.

Gospel Cummings' face was a hard mask as he holstered his six-shooter. One long step took him to the wounded man, and his arms caught Benson under the buttocks. Another step took Cummings to the door, and he threw Shorty across the yard and under the tie-rail.

"You came here with murder in your heart, and I don't aim to have you mess up my house with your cowardly blood!" Cummings said gruffly. "You ain't hurt none to speak of, but you'll never trigger another killer-gun as long as you live!"

"I'm bleeding out!" Benson screamed. "You just about cut my hand off at the wrist!"

Gospel Cummings fought hard to control his rising anger. It was not often that he lost his self-control, but the knowledge that Shorty Benson had meant to kill him in cold blood stifled the natural pity Cummings would have for any wounded man.

"Bleed out!" he rasped at the sniveling gunman. "And your blood won't be on my conscience none to speak of!"

"'Thou shalt not kill!'" Shorty Benson whined. "I heard you say so your own self. I'm bleeding out, and you won't ever get it offen yore conscience!"

"On your feet," Cummings growled. "And stay where you are. I'll wrap a rag around that hand, and help you on your bronc. You can ride into town and see Doc Brady, and you can tell him I did it!"

He strode back into his cabin and found a clean rag. He also found the bottle of Three Daisies, and after downing a stiff drink, he carried the bottle outside and poured whiskey over Shorty Benson's bleeding hand. He bound up the wounded hand, and looked about him.

"So you hid your horse out in the Devil's Graveyard," he accused Benson. "I'll walk back there with you, and you tell the rest of that 3 B outfit what happened. Start walking!"

Five minutes later Jeff Dawson rode into the little yard. He stared at Cummings, at the smoke-grimed pistol in the plainsman's holster, and asked a blunt question.

"Does that old outlaw gun shoot straight?"

"It shoots straight," Cummings growled. "That's another one I owe old Jim. That was his gun you left here, and a good thing you did."

He explained what had happened, and Jeff Dawson scowled. "If I had my way, we'd paint for war and take it to that 3 B outfit," he muttered.

"That ain't the way to do it," Cummings argued. "Time enough when they bring it to us! Besides, he like as not did this all on his own," Cummings explained. "It rankled him because I took the flat of my hand to him yesterday. He considered it a deadly insult, and he was going to wipe it out in blood."

Dawson changed the subject abruptly. "Thanks for what you said."

Cummings appeared puzzled. "What did I say?" he asked.

"About that one good reason I had for not fighting my head," Jeff explained. "Connie Brighton."

"The prettiest little filly in Arizona," Cummings said heartily.

Dawson stared at his companion. "I wonder now," he said slowly. "I wonder how much you heard when I was talking to Connie?"

"If I heard anything, I approved of it," Cummings said lamely. He picked up the whiskey bottle he had used to cleanse Shorty Benson's wound, and flung it into the brush. Then he walked into the cabin, saying he would get a hot bait of grub for supper.

Jeff Dawson watched him, and a smile came to his face for the first time since the fight back in the badlands. He rode to the little barn and stripped his riding gear, and after feeding the horses, Dawson walked to the entrance and into the burying ground.

He approached the newly mounded grave and took off his Stetson. Then he hunkered down on his boot-heels.

"Thanks for everything, old Jim," he murmured. "I'm going to try and keep my head cool, and clear your good name. Now you just take your rest and let me carry on from here!"

CHAPTER SIX

Jeff Dawson stirred restlessly as the first rays of the early sun tugged at his eyelids. Awareness came to him at once, and he awoke fully refreshed and ready for what the new day might bring. He glanced over at the opposite bunk, expecting to see Gospel Cummings still making up his sleep. But the gaunt plainsman was watching him with a smile on his bearded lips.

"Howdy, Jeff," Cummings said cheerfully. "Here it is five o'clock of the morning; soon it will be nine, and then noontime. Half the day gone, and we're not up yet!"

"Putting it that way, we better rise and shine," Jeff agreed. "I slept better last night than I have in years."

Soon they were riding open range. After a while Jeff pointed to a sagging wire fence.

"That's home," he said quietly. "Let's ride in."

Jeff Dawson swung down at the tie-rail before a neat ranch house on the Triangle D. Gospel Cummings stared at the new chintz curtains which framed the windows from the inside, and nodded his head.

Dawson dismounted and ground-tied his horse. He walked to the front door, pushed it open, and stood staring at the clean interior.

"Someone has been here," he said lamely. "Someone has cleaned the whole house!"

"Yeah," Cummings agreed. "That would like as not be Sandra Fleming, Molly Waggoner, and Connie Brighton." He stared at a piece of paper which appeared to be tacked to a panel of the door to the kitchen. "Looks like they left you a note, Jeff," he remarked carelessly.

Jeff Dawson crossed the room with a smile of anticipation on his tanned face. The smile changed to a scowl, and Cummings hurried to the cowboy's side.

"It's a warning, Gospel," Jeff muttered.

Gospel Cummings read the message slowly aloud:

"Be warned, outlaw! We know you are after the loot, but you will never live to find it. The James gang!"

"From what I heard, old Fred Haney was the last of the James gang," Cummings said slowly.

"Some of those Boyds left this warning," Dawson said savagely. "Let's ride over there to the 3 B and settle it now!"

"We don't know that it was them," Cummings objected, and then his bearded face lit up. "Tell you what we can do," he suggested. "We can take tools and mend the fence, and we are bound to see them."

Jeff Dawson scratched his curly head. "I don't see my wagon," he muttered. "We'd have to take wire and tools."

Gospel Cummings smiled. He pointed to a dust-cloud coming across the open range. "Wagon coming from the direction of the Circle F," he said.

"Ace Fleming is driving that rig," Jeff said, after a long scrutiny. "And several of his hands are riding behind the wagon."

"Ace is right neighborly," Cummings remarked. "He took your wagon and had it greased and painted. Let's ride out and give him a howdy!"

They mounted their horses and raced to meet the Circle F crew. Ace Fleming greeted the two riders with a broad grin and a cheery "Howdy," and said they'd help Jeff run his fence between the Triangle D and the 3 B graze.

"Stop off at the house first, Ace," Cummings said. "Someone left a note for Jeff, and you might have some ideas."

Fleming tooled his team into the yard, wrapped the lines around the brake-handle, and jumped to the ground. His crew of four cowboys sat their horses in the yard, and Fleming followed Cummings inside the house and stared at the note on the door.

"I've heard about that outlaw swag," Fleming said thoughtfully. "Someone wants that loot, but they don't know where it is."

"Let's read sign, even if we make most of it ourselves," Jeff Dawson said slowly. "Who shot my Dad, and who wanted to buy my Triangle D graze?"

"Terry Boyd shot old Jim," Cummings answered. "But it was Tom Boyd who made you the offer for the Triangle D!"

"I dunno," Fleming protested. "They've had three years to look for it, and it could be somebody else!"

"Shorty Benson!" Dawson guessed.

"Not him," Cummings contradicted. "Shorty couldn't have printed that note with his right hand, and he ain't left-handed."

"On top of that, he's in jail," Fleming added. "The Saint arrested him for assault with a deadly weapon; he's holding him until you ride in and sign the complaint," he told Cummings.

"I'm signing no complaint," Cummings said gruffly. "But the rest will do Shorty good. He lost some blood."

"You should have killed him, Gospel," Fleming said coldly.

Gospel Cummings turned and stared at the gambler's handsome face. Fleming nodded. "I know, old friend," he murmured. " 'Thou shalt not kill!' "

"I don't see it that way," Jeff said coldly. "Shorty Benson wasn't much better than his boss!"

"He was different," Cummings defended the 3 B cowboy. "Shorty did give me warning, and in his way, he meant to give me what he called a fighting chance. Let's get out there to our work," Cummings suggested. "There's plenty to do."

He left the house and mounted his sorrel. Fleming climbed to the driver's seat of the wagon, and the crew started across the rolling range. They reached the boundary of the 3 B in less than an hour, and Fleming stopped his team near a break in the fence.

"Someone cut that panel," he said. "How long is your line, Jeff?"

"About a mile," Dawson answered. "The Triangle D is two sections long and one section wide."

"It won't take long to make that mile section

tight," Cummings commented. He turned to stare at the Circle F crew. "Climb down and grab a wire-stretcher, cowboys," he said with a grin. "The day is past when you can do all your work from the saddle."

Gospel Cummings took a can filled with heavy staples, found a hammer in the wagon, and started to work. Three panels were replaced, and the work was finished by the middle of the afternoon.

"Horse-backers coming," Fleming warned, as he watched a small group of riders loping from the east. "Couldn't be anyone else but the 3 B crew!"

Four men raced up and slid their horses to a stop near the working crew. They were the three Boyd brothers, and Red Stang. It was Terry Boyd who directed a shouted question at Gospel Cummings.

"Did you throw down on Shorty Benson, you old pelican?"

"I did, you young squirt," Cummings answered evenly. "You taking up for him?"

"He was my saddle-pard," Red Stang interrupted quietly.

"I am a man of peace, Red," Cummings said slowly. "I never start trouble. But I've never run away from it when it was brought to me. It's your play!"

"I'll deal this hand!" Fleming said sharply. "Don't start something you can't finish, Stang. Shorty rode down to Three Points and got Gospel under his gun. He was going to kill Gospel, but

Gospel had an ace in the hole. Right now Saint John is holding your pard in the calabozo, waiting for Gospel to ride in and sign a complaint!"

Tom Boyd and his brother Dixon sat their saddles, and watched the bearded face of Gospel Cummings. Tom seemed to be digesting Fleming's statement, and finding food for thought. Dixon Boyd followed his older brother's example; the two seemed to be leaving the argument to Terry, who had shouted the beginning of a challenge at Cummings. His words and attitude would have led to an open clash with any other than a professed man of peace.

Red Stang also seemed to have changed his mind. He showed no sign of fear, but his bearing was not so truculent as when he had made his statement that Shorty Benson was his saddle-pard.

"I seldom sit in judgment on my fellow-man," Cummings said quietly. "Shorty rode down to Three Points to kill me. I had no part in Saint John's writing out that complaint!"

"You going to sign it?" Stang demanded of Cummings.

Cummings shook his head. "I shot the gun from Shorty's hand, but he won't ever trigger another cutter."

"I'm sorry I went on the prod that away, Cummings," Red Stang said quietly, and Terry Boyd stared at the tall redhead.

"I ain't eating crow!" he snarled viciously.

"Shorty Benson was working for the 3 B, and we stand behind him!"

Tom Boyd rubbed his chin and glanced at his brother Dixon. "What do you make of this?" he asked.

"Looks to me like Shorty got what was coming to him," Dixon Boyd answered thoughtfully. "He rode into town without orders, and he rode down to Three Points on his own."

Terry Boyd stared at his brothers, and his face darkened with anger. The cast in his left eye slanted upward, and he turned on Gospel Cummings with a savage curse.

"I'll stand behind Shorty!" he shouted. "I've likewise got unfinished business with you for what you did yesterday in Hell's Half Acre! You shot the hat from my head when I didn't have a gun in my hand!"

"Which saved you a fate like Shorty Benson is now suffering," Cummings answered quietly. "Even if I am not a killer like some I could mention, self-preservation is the first law of Nature!"

"Who wants to live forever?" Terry demanded hotly. "I'd rather be dead than take any more slack from an old sin-buster like you!"

"Give it to him, Gospel," Jeff Dawson told Cummings savagely.

"I'll get around to you later, cowboy," Terry Boyd promised Dawson. "I'm bringing it to you, Cummings!"

Gospel Cummings sighed. He was on the ground, and he spoke to Terry Boyd, who still sat his saddle.

"Climb down out of your hull, cowboy," he said slowly. "I don't want to shoot a horse, but we might as well get this settled!"

"Let me have him, Gospel!" Jeff Dawson pleaded. "That gun-sneak killed old Jim!"

"Keep out of this, Jeff," Cummings said quietly.

"Climb down, Terry," Dixon Boyd growled at his younger brother. "You asked for it, and you'll face it square!"

Terry Boyd dismounted just as a big man rode from a copse of alders at a dead run. There was no mistaking the burly figure of John Saint John, and he rode between Terry Boyd and Gospel Cummings.

"What's going on here?" the deputy bellowed.

Gospel Cummings remained silent, as did Terry Boyd. It was Tom Boyd who broke the silence.

"We just rode over to see who was pounding on this boundary fence," he told Saint John. "And while you're here, Gospel won't sign a complaint against Shorty Benson, so when you get back to town, turn him loose. Tell him to make tracks going away!"

Saint John turned angrily on Gospel Cummings. "You're obstructing the law!" he accused. "If you was any kind of citizen, you'd ride in and sign that complaint!"

"I'm not that kind of citizen," Cummings answered quietly. "Turn Shorty loose!"

Saint John glared at Gospel Cummings as he tugged at his long cowhorn mustaches. "I don't savvy you, Gospel," he growled, his voice heavy with exasperation. "Here's a chance for you to help the law make an example of a cold killer who plays a sneak with intent to commit cold murder. It might keep down other killings. But you go pious on me!"

"Pious is not the proper word," Cummings said stiffly. "Let's say I have no desire for revenge, and I do believe in giving a man another chance!"

The deputy swore softly and turned to Red Stang. "Your pard was asking for you, Stang," he growled. "He wants the loan of a month's pay for a riding stake. That is, unless you want to quit the country with him," he added hopefully.

"I like this country," Red Stang said lazily. He turned to Tom Boyd. "I've got a month's-pay coming, and so has Shorty," he reminded. "If you'll pay it over to the law, he can give it to Shorty for a riding stake!"

Tom Boyd dug down into his hip pocket and brought out a thick roll of paper money. He counted out eighty dollars, handed it to Saint John, and returned the roll to his pocket. "Give that to Shorty, and tell him to get long gone," Boyd said sourly. "We'll be getting back to headquarters. Come on, you rannies!"

The four 3 B men whirled their horses and raced away without another word. Jeff Dawson stared at their loping horses, and turned to study Cummings. Saint John nodded his head and spoke curtly.

"You and Terry Boyd was fixing to shoot it out," he stated. "The law would like to know why."

"It was nothing at all," Cummings murmured. "Just a little difference of opinion, you might say."

"So for one time you figured to keep Terry Boyd honest," Saint John guessed shrewdly. "You had enough witnesses!"

"That's right," Cummings agreed.

"Keep on talking," the big deputy said irritably. "What was this difference of opinion?"

"Well, you was down to the burying," Cummings answered carelessly. "You saw what went on, and you know about the ruckus in town."

"That's right, keep on talking, but don't say anything," Saint John sneered. "I asked you a straight question, and I demand a straight answer!"

Cummings shrugged and turned to Ace Fleming. "You remember what it was about?" he asked the gambler.

"Something about not turning Shorty Benson loose," Fleming said carelessly. "It didn't seem important to me, so I didn't listen very close." He turned to Jeff Dawson. "I'll have the Circle F crew move your herd over tomorrow, Jeff," he told the Triangle D cowboy.

"Thanks for everything, Ace," Dawson said gratefully.

Saint John swore angrily. "Ignore the law, you unwashed cow nurses!" he exploded. "There will come a day when you will want the law to give you a hand!"

"When that day comes, we'll ask for it," Cummings said.

"I've got law business back in town," the deputy growled. He whirled his horse and heeled the spurs home to spurt the big bay in a sudden burst of speed. Fleming watched the deputy's departure with a smile, and then he spoke thoughtfully to Cummings. "I can't quite savvy Tom Boyd," he said slowly. "He and Dix didn't side Terry one bit. What do you make of that, Gospel?"

Cummings evaded a direct answer. "Mebbe we misjudged those 3 B fellers!"

"They rode down after old Jim!" Jeff Dawson interrupted hotly. "And they killed him on a sneak!"

"You saw them kill him?" Fleming asked.

"I saw Terry Boyd do it!" Dawson almost shouted.

"Lay your hackles, son," Cummings said soothingly. "That's part of my thinking. You saw Terry shoot old Jim. Where were Tom and Dixon at the time?"

"They were up on that hog-back near Lobo's peak," Dawson answered savagely.

"That's almost a mile from where old Jim was shot," Cummings said slowly.

"It don't make much difference," Dawson argued angrily. "If either one of them had seen old Jim first, they'd have done what their brother did!"

"That's where I think you are wrong, Jeff," Cummings said. "Tom Boyd ain't noways like Terry, and Dix takes a lot after Tom. Tom won't back up a step when he thinks he is right, but he won't back up another feller if he thinks that hombre is wrong!"

"You sticking up for them 3 B bosses?" Jeff asked thinly.

"Looks like," Cummings agreed. "I've known Tom Boyd for a long time. Now you do some thinking back, Jeff. Didn't Tom tell Terry not more than fifteen minutes ago that this time he would have to face what he started . . . alone?"

Jeff Dawson rubbed his chin. "Reckon he did," he admitted. "He as good as told Terry that he was on his own. Then Saint John rode in and spoiled the play."

"For which I am thankful," Cummings murmured. "I hate and despise the ways of war! But we were talking about Tom Boyd. I still claim that Tom would have given old Jim a square chance if he had met him first!"

"But they were riding after old Jim," Dawson snarled angrily.

"That's right," Cummings agreed. "Now look at it this way, Jeff. Say you had lost a payroll of two thousand dollars. You'd try to do something about it, wouldn't you?"

"Jim never did that job!" Jeff declared passionately.

"You and I know that, but what about Tom and Dix Boyd?"

"Gospel made a point there, Jeff," Fleming cut in. "Don't you see it? Looks to me like Tom and Dixon Boyd don't hold with everything Terry has done. They even forced him to face Gospel for a showdown!"

"I'll face that killer some day!" Jeff Dawson promised grimly. "When I do, I won't throw off my shot!"

"Well, may that day be long deferred," Cummings said hopefully. "Let's leave it the way it is for now, Jeff."

"I made old Jim a promise!" Jeff Dawson muttered. "I'll keep that promise if I have to play it lone-handed!"

"Which you won't," Cummings assured the angry youngster. "How long have Shorty Benson and Red Stang been on the 3 B payroll?" he asked Fleming.

Ace Fleming glanced at one of his crew. "You know how long, Charley?" he asked.

Charley Bailey was a tall strapping cowboy of perhaps twenty-four. He had not spoken a word during the arguments; cowboys learn early to listen well, and speak when they have something to say.

"Little over seven months," Bailey answered.

"Where are they from?" Fleming asked.

"They rode up here from the Nations," Bailey said slowly.

"Oklahoma is a pretty big place," Fleming murmured.

"That Red Stang is a mighty good shot with a six-pistol," Bailey offered carelessly. "From what I gathered, he sold his gun more than once down there in the Nations."

Dawson listened intently. He remembered the fist fight with the lanky 3 B cowboy, and then he saw Cummings watching his face.

"I'm faster than Stang with a cutter," Dawson said gruffly.

Charley Bailey shook his head doubtfully, but he did not speak.

"You think Red has Jeff faded with his hardware?" Ace Fleming asked the big cowboy.

"I never saw Jeff work none with his tools," Bailey answered bluntly. "But I was riding with Stang one day out close to the lavas. A big old diamond-back slithered out of the grass, and Stang cut that serpent's head off with one shot before I had cleared leather with my smoke-pole. Fastest shooting I ever saw, and the straightest!"

Jeff Dawson looked thoughtful, and Gospel

Cummings smiled. Ace Fleming tugged at his clipped mustache and spoke slowly.

"Must be a lot of good in that red-headed puncher," he said quietly. "He and Jeff had a fist fight, and Red never made a pass for his hardware. He took his beating like a man, which is more than I can say for his saddle-pard."

"And Stang didn't side his pard when Shorty rode down to kill me on a sneak," Cummings said. "Then he gives his riding pay to his pard, but looks like he don't want no more truck with him."

"He leaves me alone, I'll mind my own business," Jeff Dawson said quietly. "But you gents are overlooking one thing."

"Such as . . . ?" Fleming asked.

"Red Stang and Terry Boyd," Dawson continued. "They seemed to understand each other, and those other two Boyds didn't seem to know the score."

"I noticed that," Cummings said slowly.

"I want to thank all you hands for helping me," Jeff Dawson said earnestly. "I couldn't have made it alone, and I know it. I will always be in your debt for what you did for me, Ace."

"Think nothing of it," Fleming said with a smile. "We try to be neighborly here in the Strip; we cattlemen have got to stick together."

"Another thing," Dawson said, and he swallowed hard. "Thank Sandra and Molly for fixing up my house for me."

"You mean you don't want me to thank Connie Brighton?" Fleming tormented the Triangle D cowboy. "It was Connie who got Sandra and Molly to help her fix your *casa.*"

"Mebbe Jeff wants to thank Connie himself," Cummings teased.

"Yeah, that's right," Dawson said slowly. "I'll thank Connie myself, the next time I see her."

"Make it tomorrow night," Fleming suggested. "Sandra is giving a dance at the Circle F to welcome a wandering cowboy back home. A waddy by the name of Jefferson Davis Dawson!"

CHAPTER SEVEN

Ace Fleming's Circle F ranch house was brilliantly lighted for the welcoming-home dance. Riders were arriving from all of the neighboring ranches, and the musicians were tuning their instruments in the large living room. Sandra, a pretty woman in her late twenties, ran to greet Gospel Cummings as he came into the room with Jeff Dawson. She put her arms around the gaunt plainsman and kissed him affectionately.

"I'm mighty glad you came, Gospel," she said happily. "And I want the first dance with you."

"I'm not so much on the Doe-si-doe any more, but how can I refuse?" Cummings answered with a smile.

Sandra smiled and then drew closer and whispered a question. "Is Jeff feeling better now?"

"He's kinda mixed up in his mind," Cummings answered guardedly. "He thinks a heap of Connie Brighton."

"And she talks of nothing else but Jeff," Sandra confided.

"When did you girls leave the Triangle D after you fixed up Jeff's house?" Cummings asked curiously.

"About eight that night," Sandra answered. "Ace rode over to see us home. Why do you ask, Gospel?"

"Someone was there after you left," Cummings explained. "Left a note pinned to a door for Jeff."

"More trouble?" Sandra whispered.

Cummings nodded his head. "Looks like," he admitted. His eyes narrowed as Red Stang came into the room, dressed in his cowboy best. "You invited the 3 B outfit?" Cummings asked.

"Not personally, but everyone was invited," Sandra answered. "You know how cowboys are when there's a dance."

Jeff Dawson was talking to Connie Brighton, and he was holding her hand. "Can I have the first dance?" he asked hopefully.

Connie nodded. "And the last, if you like," she promised.

"That means I can take you home," Jeff said with a happy smile. "I must be living right since I came in out of the tangles!"

"Try to forget those years," Connie urged. "You are a cattleman now, Jeff."

"I've dreamed about my own little spread for years," Jeff admitted. "You have a lot of time to think about things back yonder in the badlands where you don't see much company. I still can't believe that I own a little outfit of my own."

"It's true," Connie assured him. "Look; I'll pinch you to convince you it is not just a dream!"

"I dreamed of a lot of things," Jeff murmured. "Things I can't talk much about until I get the Triangle D started."

Red Stang approached the pair, and he smiled at Connie. "Please, can I have the second dance?" he asked. "I know that Triangle D waddy has spoken for the first."

"You may," Connie agreed. "Do you boys know each other?"

"We've met," Jeff said bluntly.

"He whipped me with his maulies," Red Stang said with a wide smile. "He jumped me so fast and hit me so often, I thought he was twins!"

"And there's no hard feelings?" Connie asked wonderingly.

"Shucks no," Stang said slowly. "A cowboy will fight for money or marbles, or he will fight for fun and frolic. No hard feelings, and here's my hand on it, Dawson!"

Jeff Dawson stiffened, and then he accepted the proffered hand. "No hard feelings on my part either," he said earnestly.

Red Stang looked at Jeff Dawson with a level

gaze. He started to speak, changed his mind, and drew a deep breath.

"You was going to say?" Dawson prompted.

"Well, I was thinking that you're short-handed on the Triangle D," Stang began hesitantly. "I'm a fair cow-camp cook, a top hand with horses and cattle, and I'd make you a good hand at the same money the 3 B was paying me."

Jeff Dawson stared at Stang, trying to read what was going on behind the tall redhead's blue eyes. Red Stang smiled boyishly, and then he shrugged one shoulder. "I'm sorry about that little run-in, Dawson," he said manfully. "I changed my mind about several things. I'll say the same to Gospel Cummings when I see him."

Jeff Dawson frowned. Was this a plant to place a 3 B man where he could report to the Boyds? "I'll think it over, Red," Dawson said quietly. "I'll let you know before the dance is over."

The three-piece orchestra struck up with "Buffalo Gals," and Jeff claimed Connie for the first dance. As they whirled across the floor to complete a square, Red Stang sought another partner.

Gospel Cummings strolled across the room to talk to Cole Brighton, Connie's father and owner of the big Box B outfit. The old cattleman was a tall and vigorous man in his late fifties. He greeted Cummings cordially, and jerked his head towards Connie and Jeff Dawson.

"They make a handsome pair," Brighton said proudly. "I hope that Dawson boy settles down and makes a solid citizen."

"He's bound to do it," Cummings said confidently. "I knew his Dad when old Jim was Jeff's age. When Jim got married, he settled down and did right well."

"Young Jeff ain't of age yet," Brighton grunted. "He won't be thinking of marriage for quite a while."

"You want to bet?" Cummings asked with a slow smile.

The music stopped, and Red Stang claimed Connie for the second dance. Cummings nudged Cole Brighton when Jeff Dawson started toward them. Dawson took a chair near the two men.

"I've been thinking, Gospel," Dawson said hesitantly. "I'm going to need some help on the Triangle D. Would you consider some kind of partnership with me? There's room enough for both of us."

Gospel Cummings shook his head. "Thanks, Jeff," he said gratefully. "But you know how it is. I'm the boss of Hell's Half Acre, and that's where my work is. You need a younger man."

"There will be plenty of work," Jeff agreed. "Right now the Triangle D is just about a two-man spread, the way old Jim and I had planned. I'd rather have you than any younger man I know."

"I don't do much cow-work any more, Jeff,"

Cummings said slowly. "I make a hand once in a while when Ace or Cole Brighton gets pressed for help, but then I go back to Three Points where I belong."

"Your experience would be worth a lot," Dawson persisted.

"You can always have that, for what it might be worth," Cummings answered slowly. "And it won't be for sale."

"A feller asked me for a job, Gospel," Dawson admitted. "But I'm not sure."

Cummings appeared surprised. "Must have happened recent," he said slowly. "Who was this cowhand?"

"Red Stang!"

Gospel Cummings jerked up with a startled look in his brown eyes. Then he relaxed and stroked his silky brown beard.

"Red is a good hand, but we don't know much about him," he said slowly. "Far as that goes, we don't know much about any wandering cowpoke who drifts in looking for a riding job. You going to take him on?"

"I wanted to talk to you about it," Dawson said hesitantly. "He offered me his hand in front of Connie; said he had no hard feelings because I had bested him in that skull-and-knuckle ruckus."

"He'd make a better friend than an enemy . . . if he was a friend," Cummings remarked. "Tell you what, Jeff. I'll stay on with you a few days, and you put Red on the payroll. I'll watch him close, and we will soon find out what kind of critter he is."

"That sounds sensible to me," Brighton interrupted. "I couldn't help hearing the talk, and that Red Stang is a good cowhand."

Red Stang escorted Connie to the place where the three men were talking, and thanked her for the dance. Jeff had asked for the next dance, but he spoke to Stang before taking to the dance floor.

"You're on the Triangle D payroll, starting tomorrow, Red," he told the tall cowboy.

"Well, thanks, Boss," Red Stang answered with a grin. "I've got my soogans on a spare horse out in the corral. You see, I quit the 3 B this afternoon."

Gospel Cummings and Cole Brighton exchanged glances. Jeff Dawson looked surprised, but he swept Connie in his arms as the music started. Cummings spoke quietly to Stang.

"Did you have any trouble with Terry Boyd?" he asked.

The tall redhead frowned and stared at the bearded plainsman.

"I had words with Tom Boyd," he answered frankly. "It was on account of Shorty Benson."

Gospel Cummings frowned thoughtfully. He remembered how Stang had refused to back up Terry Boyd, and he knew Terry's temper. Tom Boyd was usually quiet and self-controlled, and Red Stang was a good working cowboy.

"Tom Boyd is the boss on the 3 B," Stang said, after a pause. "He does the hiring and firing, and keeps the books. We had a few words, and I just asked him to write out my time."

"Sorry I had to cripple Benson that away," Cummings said with sincerity. "You and Shorty are not much alike, Red."

"I met him down in Tulsa," Stang said slowly. "We were both on the loose, so we just rode together. But Shorty is leaving town, and I'm staying here."

"Do you like Jeff Dawson?" Cummings asked bluntly.

Red Stang nodded as a grin spread over his long bony face. "I like him," he said slowly. "He's the first waddy who has whipped me in quite a spell. And when you can't whip 'em, jine 'em. On top of that, I need a job."

"So you've got one," Cummings closed the subject. "You do the right thing with Jeff, he'll do the square thing with you. Now I have to see a man about a dog."

Cummings stretched to his feet and crossed the crowded room. He walked outside, stepped behind a string of horses tied at the rail, and reached for his right coat tail.

He was wiping his beard with the back of his hand when a single horse-backer rode into the big Circle F yard. Cummings frowned when Terry Boyd swung down and ground-tied his 3 B horse.

Boyd walked to the open front door, and Cummings remained behind the horses. He reached to his saddlebags on old Fred, and slipped his old Peacemaker forty-five into his holster.

Terry Boyd was armed, but he did not enter the house. He jerked his head at someone inside, and after a moment Red Stang came outside.

"You wanted to see me?" the tall redhead asked.

Terry Boyd stepped away from the door. "What's the idea of rolling your bed and quitting the 3 B without telling me?" he demanded.

"Tom Boyd said I was all through at the 3 B," Stang answered. "I was going to quit anyhow."

"Traveling with Shorty, mebbe?" Boyd asked.

Stang shook his head. "I'm staying here," he answered. "I've already got me another job, and one I'll like better."

"With who?" Boyd demanded harshly.

"Look, mister," Stang answered quietly, but his tone was cross, "since when you got a license to ride over here to a celebration and put me on the griddle?"

"Since you quit the 3 B!" Boyd answered bluntly. "Who you going to work for?"

"It ain't none of your business, but I signed on with the Triangle D," Stang answered. "And I fight for the iron that pays me my wages," he added.

"Uh, uh," Terry Boyd contradicted. "You'll fight

for the man who pays you the most money. I'll pay you another fifty a month to keep me posted."

"That's more than I got making a working hand on the 3 B," Stang said coldly. "What's the joker, Boyd?"

"Money makes money," Terry Boyd answered with a chuckle. "I want to make some fast dinero, and you can help me. All you have to do is keep your eyes and ears open, and your mouth closed about me."

"I never vent another man's brand," Stang said quietly. "I never took part in a stick-up, and I don't want fast money bad enough to ride outside the law."

"Which I'm not asking you to do," Boyd answered. "I'm offering you an easy fifty a month for information I need!"

Gospel Cummings crouched behind the horses, listening intently. He caught his breath sharply when Red Stang spoke in a whisper.

"I'll take it, Boyd. I know what you're looking for!"

"I'll see you every day or so over by that first panel in the fence Dawson mended today," Boyd said guardedly. "I'm not welcome here, so I'll be riding along!"

Boyd mounted his horse and rode into the darkness. Red Stang walked back into the house.

Gospel Cummings was not often fooled in his judgment of men, and he admitted that he had liked Red Stang. With Stang planted on the Triangle D, in the pay of Terry Boyd . . . Gospel Cummings shook his head to acknowledge that he was puzzled. He decided to wait for a day or two, and see what would happen, and after hiding his six-shooter in his saddle-bags, Cummings went back to the house.

The dancers were swirling about the floor, and some of the older men were gathered in the kitchen where Sandra Fleming had provided a bountiful feast. Ace was helping his wife, but he came to Cummings' side as the tall man of peace entered the kitchen.

"Anything wrong, Gospel?" Fleming asked quietly.

"I can't be sure, Ace," Cummings answered. "What do you think of Red Stang?"

"There's a job here on the Circle F for him whenever he wants it," Fleming answered promptly. "Why do you ask?"

"He's signed up to ride for the Triangle D," Cummings told the gambler. "And he just talked to Terry Boyd outside the house."

"Boyd rode over here after what happened yesterday?" Fleming murmured. "What did he want?"

"He's paying Red fifty a month to keep him posted," Cummings explained, and he did not require a promise of secrecy from Fleming.

"It's about that outlaw loot," Fleming said slowly.

"Yeah," Cummings agreed. "Now where does that put Red Stang?"

"Let it ride for a time, Gospel," Fleming suggested. "Watch Stang close, and you'll learn more about him."

Red Stang wandered into the kitchen, and the two men stopped talking. Sandra Fleming invited Stang to help himself, and the tall cowboy accepted the invitation eagerly. Then he saw Gospel Cummings and came over with his plate.

"I'll ride back with you to the Triangle D, Gospel," he invited himself. "Jeff is going to take Connie Brighton home."

"I'm heading back soon," Cummings answered carelessly. "I thought you yearlings would stay till the last cat was hung."

"I've had enough dancing," Stang answered shortly.

"What for kind of hombre is Terry Boyd, when you get to know him well?" Cummings asked suddenly.

Stang turned swiftly. "I reckon he's all right," he answered carelessly. "I did my work and didn't mix much with the bosses."

"But Terry mixed more with the crew than either Tom or Dixon," Cummings prompted. "Mebbe it was because Terry rode down to Texas and in the Nations occasionally. That way he would meet more people, and he'd broaden himself some."

"Yeah, what you might call democratic," Stang agreed. "But I never had much to do with him."

"He didn't like it much when you refused to back up his play," Cummings murmured slowly. "I looked for you and him to have some trouble, but that's your own affair."

"I didn't have any trouble with him," Stang answered without hesitation. "I don't think Tom liked it much because I drew some back pay and sent it to Shorty Benson for a traveling stake. Tom didn't like what Benson did, and he didn't like me siding him, as far as I went."

"Seems to me you were on the outs with both Tom and Terry," Cummings made conversation.

"Tom ain't hard to understand," Stang offered. "But you were talking about Terry Boyd."

"I mean, he's not much like his brother Tom," Cummings continued. "I'd say that Tom Boyd is the balance wheel on that outfit."

"He's got a level head," Stang agreed. "Matter of fact, Terry Boyd is in debt to Tom and Dixon. He lost a lot of money gambling, and he don't own much of the 3 B."

"Well, that's his own business," Cummings said with a shrug. "Every man has his failings. What part of Texas do you hail from?"

"I didn't say I was from Texas," Stang answered defensively.

"Southern part," Cummings said quietly. "Down around the Big Bend."

"I've been around Austin and Amarillo," Stang admitted. "But then, I've been over most of Texas."

"Terry Boyd traveled down that way for quite a while," Cummings said, as though he was making conversation. "He just came back here about a year ago, and Tom didn't like it much at the time."

Stang changed the subject abruptly. "How many head of stock does Jeff run?"

Just then Jeff Dawson came into the big kitchen with Connie, and Jeff excused himself and came over to Stang and Cummings.

"I'm going to ride home with Connie," he explained. "You fellers don't need to wait up for me, but I'll see you at breakfast."

"Keep your eyes open when you ride back alone," Cummings warned. "Stay away from the 3 B, just in case Terry Boyd might be out riding tonight."

Jeff Dawson smiled and jerked his head toward Stang. "Red would know where to look and what to do if I got dry-gulched," he said.

"That's whatever," Stang agreed promptly. "If Terry Boyd pulls a sneak on you, Gospel and I will ride gun-sign on him, and I won't throw off my shots!"

"That ain't the way," Cummings objected. "If you wound a killer, he just might give up head and talk with his mouth wide open!"

He watched the face of Red Stang as he spoke,

but the tall redhead showed no surprise. He was watching Connie Brighton as the pretty girl talked to Sandra Fleming, and when Jeff joined Connie, Cummings nudged Stang gently.

"I believe I'll get on back to the Triangle D, Red. You ready to go?"

"I'm ready," Stang answered. "I'm going to try to earn my pay on the Triangle D, Gospel. You know that, don't you?"

"Sure, sure," Cummings answered. "Let's make tracks for our bunks. This shindig will last till the crack of dawn, and I'm not as young as I used to be by at least twenty years!"

CHAPTER EIGHT

Connie Brighton smiled happily as she rode across the open range with Jeff. A faint streak of light showed in the east; the couple had danced all night. Cole Brighton had departed at midnight for the Box B, shortly after Gospel had left the Circle F with Red Stang.

"It's good to be back home again," Dawson said gratefully. "It got mighty lonesome back there on Lobo's Peak."

"It must be terrible to be hunted," Connie agreed. "But now you are home again, and that is all a thing of the past."

"There was so little for a kid to do," Jeff complained. "So I kept thinking of the Triangle D, and mostly I was thinking about you, and wondering what you were doing."

"We were both growing up," Connie said gravely. "I was finishing school, and thinking some of going to college."

Jeff Dawson appeared alarmed. "That would take you another four years," he protested. "I couldn't do without you that long!"

Connie pressed his hand and made no reply. They were skirting a bosque of trees near a flowing creek, and Connie Brighton shivered slightly. "That leads back to the badlands," she whispered.

"Stand them hosses!" a gruff voice interrupted sharply. "Keep them hands high, yearling!"

Jeff Dawson's right hand started for his pistol, but he quickly changed his mind and raised both hands to a level with his shoulders when he saw four masked men covering him with cocked six-shooters.

"I've got little money on me," Dawson said quietly.

"We'll take it," a bearded ruffian answered with a sneer. "Ride up there and take his hardware, Joe," he told one of his companions.

Jeff Dawson jerked when he felt the twitch which emptied his holster. A gun probed his spine instantly, and a hoarse voice spoke a warning. "Make a move, and I'll empty your saddle and dump your carcass into Lost River!"

"My wallet is in my left hip pocket," Dawson said slowly. "Take it, and let us ride on!"

"I'll give the orders," the bearded leader growled. "You and the gal is taking a little ride with us. We want to talk some where we won't be interrupted."

Connie gasped and protested. "My father will be worried about me," she said. "He is Cole Brighton, of the Box B!"

"Let the old mosshead worry," the bearded leader said roughly. "Bend the lead, Joe. You two pilgrims follow Joe. The rest of us will bring up the drag, and don't try to make a break!"

"Do like he says," Jeff told Connie quietly.

"That's showing savvy," the bearded man praised quietly.

"Strangers in these parts, ain't you?" Jeff asked quietly. "I don't remember seeing you before."

"That makes us even," the captor answered gruffly. "But I've heard about you, which gives me a small edge."

Jeff stared at the bearded face. "Who told you about me?"

"A feller who knows you," the ruffian answered vaguely. "Now you stir up them hosses and ride along."

The man called Joe rode ahead. Connie and Jeff followed, and the other three riders closed in and brought up the rear. They rode for an hour, and just as dawn was breaking, the horses climbed a steep trail and entered a big cave.

Jeff Dawson caught his breath sharply. He was familiar with the badlands, but Connie seemed bewildered. "This is Lost River Cave," Jeff explained. "You remember where the river gets lost and flows underground back yonder?" Connie nodded, too frightened to speak. "It comes out again in this cave," Jeff explained. "Then it wanders down into a big valley."

"You learned the country right well when you and your old man was on the dodge," the bearded man said with a coarse laugh. "You and the gal light down and rest yore saddles!"

"What about the rest of us, Ben?" one of the guards asked.

"Joe Stevens stays here with me to guard the prisoners," Whiskers answered. "My name is Ben Stokes," he told Jeff. "Mean anything to you?"

"The Stokes gang! I heard you fellers operated down in Texas and Oklahoma."

"Lots of owl-hooters operate in the Nations," Stokes said with a short laugh.

"I can't see what good we will do you," Dawson argued desperately. "I'm not on the dodge any more, and I never was an owl-hooter."

"You'd mebbe so make a good one," Stokes said with a grin. "Of course you're a mite young yet, but you'll grow up one of these days."

"I won't grow much bigger," Jeff answered quietly. "All I can do now is grow older, and from what I learned back in the tangles, I don't want any more of the same."

"Sometimes a feller don't have much choice that way," Stokes said grimly. "You and your old man didn't have a chance to take your druthers, from what I heard."

"Texas is a big place." Dawson changed the subject. "And there's more cattle and money down there than there is up here."

"That's right," Stokes agreed. "But we needed a rest from robbing trains and the like. So we came up here to make a try at that loot the James boys hid out in these parts."

"Those other two will be Ad Cross and Tod Werner," Dawson said slowly. "The law will be looking for you!"

"The law has been looking for us for years," Stokes said with a shrug. "We carry our own law in our holsters!"

Connie Brighton sat down on a limestone pillar which had fallen on its side. A small fire was burning at the back of the cave; the flickering flames threw shadows and light on glistening stalactites which hung from the high ceiling.

Jeff Dawson sat down beside Connie, and Ben Stokes studied the pair. "Cole Brighton's gal, eh?" he said thoughtfully. "That old he will pay a pretty penny to get you back again!"

"So you make war on women," Dawson said

scathingly. "Do what you want with me, but let Connie ride back home!"

"I take what I want!" Stokes answered arrogantly. "What are you going to do about it?"

Jeff Dawson seethed with anger. There was little he could do, but he whispered to Connie, "Don't worry, Gospel will read the sign!"

"What's that?" Stokes demanded.

"I told her not to worry," Dawson answered without hesitation. "She knows nothing about the James loot."

"But you do," Stokes said with an evil smile. "Whereabouts is that cave located on your Triangle D spread?"

"I wish I knew," Dawson answered honestly. "Like you know, I just came in out of the tangles after my Dad was killed."

"Did Terry Boyd find the loot?" Stokes asked savagely.

"If he did, I know nothing about it," Dawson said slowly. "I don't believe anyone ever found the loot."

"Don't feed me any of that hog-wash!" Stokes said angrily. "You and your old man had plenty of time on your hands. You know where the loot is, and you better give up head and start talking."

"I don't know any more about it than you do," Dawson insisted stubbornly. "You mentioned Terry Boyd. He had more time and opportunity to search for the loot than I did."

"I'll ask him," Stokes promised grimly. "But I've got me an idea that you know more about that loot than you want to admit."

"Where does Terry Boyd fit into this picture?" Dawson asked.

"I didn't say he fitted," Stokes growled.

"Like you mentioned, a feller learns to read sign out in the badlands, when he's on the dodge," Dawson reminded. "I never did like Terry Boyd, and he likes me even less."

"That much I know," Stokes agreed.

The other two men came back to the fire, after leading the horses to a hidden recess farther back in the cave. They took seats on bedrolls and listened to the talk.

"Jim Dawson was an owl-hooter the same as us," Stokes said more quietly. "We found sign where you and him had been digging all over the Triangle D!"

"We did no digging," Dawson answered, and he seemed puzzled. "Where did you find fresh sign?"

"In five places," Stokes answered. "Every one between little hills."

"I haven't had time to ride around," Dawson stated truthfully. "I can't help you in any way. Better change your mind and let Connie and me ride on out and we'll keep still about meeting you!"

Stokes threw back his head and laughed boisterously. "Just like that," he sneered.

"Look, Stokes," Dawson said earnestly. "You don't know these cattlemen up here in the Strip. Every cowman in the Strip will ride to hunt you down. They won't take any rest until they rescue Connie!"

"That gives me an idea," Stokes muttered. "They won't shoot too much if they do find us, as long as we hold the gal. Put a piggin'-string on her wrists, Joe. If Dawson goes on the prod, I'll drill him!"

"Hold him under your cutter, and I'll hobble him first," Joe Stevens suggested. "That way you won't have to kill him."

Jeff Dawson clenched his teeth, but there was nothing he could do. He stared into the bore of Stokes' forty-five Colt, and Joe Stevens slipped a piggin'-string around his wrists; bound them behind Dawson's back. Then he bound Connie Brighton, who gasped and lowered her head.

"There ain't as much room to hide up here in the Strip as there was down in Texas," Dawson told the outlaw leader.

"You and your old man did all right," Stokes reasoned.

"The law wasn't really looking for us," Dawson explained. "None of the cattlemen were trying to find us, except the 3 B outfit. But every outfit around here will be trying to smoke you out,"

"We didn't leave any sign," Stokes said quietly. "You, Dawson. You'll either tell us where that loot is, or we'll dump you in the deep river. If old man Brighton sends a gang up here, we'll do likewise with his gal. Now you two think it over while me and the boys get breakfast. Joe, you stay on guard!"

"What will we do?" Connie whispered to Jeff, when the three men went to the fire and dipped stew from a big kettle.

"We'll save our strength and wait," Dawson whispered. "Gospel Cummings can read sign where other men would never see any. I brushed my horse against the brush, and Gospel will follow the trail."

Connie shuddered. "Do you think they will kill us?" she whispered.

Dawson did not answer at once. He was listening to a dull distant rumble, and Connie heard it too.

"That's Lost River," he whispered. "Don't worry, honey. It will take time for them to send word to your father, and you will be safe for a while!"

"But what about you?" the girl asked anxiously.

Jeff Dawson shrugged. "I'm used to it," he said slowly. "I was hiding out for nearly three years. I know the Triangle D, and mebbe I can make a deal with Ben Stokes to help him look for the loot."

"You telling the filly how much you love her?" Joe Stevens asked with a sneer.

"That's right," Dawson answered. "We were going to be married!"

Connie Brighton gasped and then drew closer to Dawson. "We were," she whispered.

"Now ain't that a shame?" Stevens murmured. "We ride in here and bust up all your plans. They ain't no justice, seems as though."

"But there is," Jeff Dawson answered quickly. "I was on the owl-hoot trail for three years, and I was cleared when Dad was killed. That's proof enough that there is justice in these parts!"

"And what did it get you?" the outlaw asked. "You're right back here in the badlands where you started!"

Ben Stokes walked up to the pair and wiped his mouth with the back of one big hand. "Have you decided to play it my way?" he asked.

"Yeah." Jeff surprised Stokes with his answer. "I know of several old caves on the Triangle D, and I could lead you to them."

"Quit stalling for time!" Stokes answered bluntly. "You and your old man found that loot. I want to know where it is!"

"It might have been found," Dawson said. "Terry Boyd has been looking for it!"

"Mebbe he's double-crossed us, Ben," Stevens interrupted. "Mebbe Boyd found the loot, and brought us in to take the blame for him!"

"He wouldn't dare take a chance," Stokes said quietly. "Terry Boyd knows what would happen to him if he tried to run a blazer on us."

"But he isn't wanted, and you are," Dawson

reminded the outlaw. "It would be just like him to lay back in the brush and shoot you out of the saddle like he did my Dad."

Ben Stokes furrowed his brow and then shook his head. "He wouldn't dare take a chance," he said positively. "We've got that 3 B payroll robbery on him, and he knows it!"

Jeff Dawson leaned forward, listening intently. Old history was being brought to light, and Ben Stokes noticed his interest.

"Not that it matters, but Terry Boyd rigged that payroll stick-up," Stokes said with a grin. "Take a good look at Joe Stevens yonder. Does he look familiar to you?"

"I never saw him before," Dawson answered.

"Say he was dressed up in your old man's clothes," Stokes suggested. "With a mask on his face, and stradling a Triangle D cayuse!"

Jeff Dawson stared at Stevens, and the truth struck him like a flash of heat lighting.

"You mean Stevens held up that 3 B cowboy, and took the payroll!" he said slowly. "That job put me and Dad on the owl-hoot, and left the Triangle D for Terry Boyd!"

"Well, it didn't do you much good," Stokes answered with a short laugh. "Now I don't cotton much to a gent who will pull a blazer like that one, and mebbe we could work better with you."

"What's your proposition, Stokes?" Dawson asked the bearded outlaw. "At least I can listen."

"I believe we can use you, yearling," Stokes said. "We will watch Terry Boyd and his brothers. You can tell us where to look for a likely cave on the Triangle D. We ought to turn up something, and we can always get ten thousand from Cole Brighton for the gal!"

"I won't play it that way," Dawson declared stubbornly. "Tell you what I'll do, Stokes. Let Connie ride out and I'll sell every head of cattle I own to pay you the difference. I can mebbe so raise about eight thousand dollars!"

"It's an idea," Stokes admitted. "But eight thousand ain't a drop in the bucket compared to that loot the James boys hid out here somewhere."

"My father will pay you the ransom," Connie spoke up hopefully. "Provided I am not harmed in any way!"

"He will pay, or you might get worse than harmed!" Stokes threatened. "Untie her, and let her write a note to her old man, Joe!"

Joe Stevens released the girl and handed her a cheap tablet and a pencil. Jeff Dawson brooded in silence, and seemed miles away. Ben Stokes watched the cowboy, and spoke grimly.

"I know how you feel, Dawson," he surprised Jeff. "It was Terry Boyd who killed your Pa!"

Jeff Dawson changed instantly. His young face grew bleak with a rage he had tried to control, but which now broke its bounds.

"He did worse than kill old Jim!" Dawson corrected. "He murdered him, and he never gave Dad a chance!"

"So you better play along with us," Stokes suggested. "If Terry Boyd pulled a whizzer like that one time, he will try it again. You can't teach an old dog new tricks!"

"So you better watch yourself," Dawson warned. "You can't trust him any further than you could throw a range bull by the tail!"

"We could mebbe fix it for you to get Terry Boyd where you'd want him," Stokes suggested.

"I'll settle with him!" Dawson swore savagely. "I'll get him if it costs me the Triangle D, and everything in the world!"

"That's telling 'em." Ben Stokes applauded. "Terry Boyd sent for us to come up here. Don't know where he got the thousand dollars he sent me, and I don't care!"

Jeff Dawson leaped to his feet. "Untie me, Stokes!" he pleaded. "I'll give you my word to sell my stock and give you every dollar. Terry Boyd collected a thousand dollar reward for killing my Dad!"

"I'll think it over, Dawson," Stokes promised. "How you coming with that note, gal?" he asked Connie Brighton. "Read it to me."

Connie glanced at Dawson, cleared her throat, and began to read the note she had written.

Dear Dad:

Jeff and I were caught by four outlaws. They will

kill me unless you pay them ten thousand dollars. Please leave the money in that line shack near Hunter's Springs tonight at twelve. Tell no one if you want to see me alive. Connie.

"That's a top hand job," Stokes praised. He turned to Tod Werner and spoke sharply. "Gear your horse and see that old man Cole Brighton gets this note," he ordered.

As Werner took the note and left for his horse, Stokes spoke to Cross and Stevens. "You boys turn in and get some sleep," he told them. "I'll watch the prisoners."

"What about Terry Boyd, Ben?" Stevens asked. "You think he's double-crossing us?"

"What do you think would happen to him if he did?" Stokes asked lazily, but his right hand caressed the grips of his gun.

"Let's take the ten thousand and get long gone," Stevens suggested. "Nobody knows for sure that the James boys really hid that loot around here!"

"I'll do the thinking for this owl-hoot outfit!" Stokes said harshly. "On top of that, we can take up the offer Dawson made!"

"I'll sell my stock to Ace Fleming and bring you the money myself!" Dawson promised eagerly.

"We'll see," Stokes temporized. "I've got a handful of good cards, and I'm going to play them." He turned as Werner led a big gray gelding from the back of the cave, and after Werner had ridden down the trail, Cross and Stevens yawned and said they'd turn in and make up their sleep. "Tie the gal up first!" Stokes barked at Stevens. "Looks like I have to do all the thinking for this outfit!"

Joe Stevens slipped the piggin'-string around Connie's wrists, and made his ties. When he had retreated to the darker recesses of the cave, Connie leaned against Jeff and closed her eyes.

"Dad will raise the money," she whispered confidently. "Perhaps Stokes will let us ride out together."

"I've got no claim on that treasure," Jeff said in a low whisper. "If I knew where it was, I'd tell Stokes for the chance to square myself with Terry Boyd!"

"I've got ears like a bat," Ben Stokes said quietly. "I believe you are telling the truth, kid!"

Jeff Dawson jerked erect. "So help me!" he said clearly. "I've no idea where the loot is hidden!"

"You'd never make a top hand owl-hooter, Dawson," Stokes said bluntly. "You stick too close to the truth, and sometimes it don't pay. There's not much honor among thieves, and most of us know it!"

"Take the money and ride on back to Texas," Connie urged. "I'm sure my father will pay, and Jeff will keep his word about selling his cattle and giving you the money!"

"Well, cut my cinchas," Stokes murmured, and then he shrugged angrily. "I never felt this way about a deal before. After what they did to you, kid, you still want to stick to the straight and narrow. You almost have me thinking I could find a new place and do the same thing!"

"You could, Stokes," Dawson said positively.

"I'll give it some thinking," Stokes promised. "Now you better try and get some sleep, and you better be right about Cole Brighton raising that *dinero*."

CHAPTER NINE

Gospel Cummings awoke as the first fugitive ray of sunlight touched his eyelids He glanced over at the bunk Jeff Dawson slept in. The bunk was empty, and Cummings slid his feet to the floor and called to Red Stang, who was sleeping on a low leather-covered couch.

"Rise and shine, Red! The boss hasn't come home yet!"

Red Stang yawned and stretched his long arms over his tousled red head. "You know how it is when a young buck gets to courting," he said carelessly. "Jeff will come drooping in for breakfast."

Cummings stomped into his boots, finished dressing, and started breakfast. During the meal he kept watching the big yard, and after finishing his coffee, he pushed away from the table.

"C'mon," he said to Stang. "We're going to ride out to meet Jeff. I've got a feeling!"

Red Stang muttered crossly as he saddled his horse. The two riders left the Triangle D, and Cummings set the pace across the rangeland. An hour later they reached the forks of the trail where the badlands led off to the west, and the Box B to the east.

Gospel Cummings was following the spoor left by the horses Dawson and Connie Brighton had ridden. He stared intently when he came to a tangle of hoof-prints, and he stroked his luxuriant brown beard thoughtfully.

"They met up with other riders here," he said to Stang. "Four of them, and I don't like it none!"

"Some of the boys riding back from the dance," Stang said. "Jeff ain't going to like it if he knows we're wet-nursing him!"

"Look, I don't trust them Boyds," Cummings said sharply. He stared at the trail and rode over to a dead bush. "Look here, Red!" he called. "This is an old Injun trick. Someone bent four branches, and laid a stick down pointing up this trail leading back to the lavas!"

Red Stang stared at the sign, and scratched his red head. He dismounted suddenly and made a dive into the brush. He was holding two forty-five cartridges in his hand when he came out facing Cummings.

"What you make of this, Gospel?" he asked the older man.

Gospel Cummings stared at the loaded shells.

"Jeff and Connie rode back here with them four," he said slowly. "Looks to me like Jeff was trying to tell me something, Red. If he threw those shells away, it means he don't have any way to use 'em!"

"So they must have taken his six-shooter," Red Stang murmured.

"That's it!" Cummings said hoarsely. "Those four must have hidden here and waited for Connie and Jeff. They took his gun, and he's pointing the trail to the badlands!"

"Four men," Stang murmured thoughtfully. "They must be strangers, Gospel. Tom Boyd wouldn't let any four of his 3 B crew pull a trick like this, and Terry Boyd wouldn't trust any four of them!"

"The Boyds wouldn't take that kind of chance," Cummings said. "You seen any strangers back here recent?"

Red shook his head. "Nary," he answered. "But that don't mean much. If they didn't want to be seen, they'd stay away from the main trails."

"Let's ride a ways," Cummings grunted. "I want to read the sign. If Jeff is in trouble, he'll find a way to let me know."

They rode up the trail and into the lava badlands. Cummings pointed to another pair of cartridges just off the trail. He raised his head and listened intently. "Hossbacker coming this way!" he whispered to Stang. "You take to the brush over yonder to the right; I'll ride in here to the left. Keep your gun handy!"

The minutes ticked away, and then the click of a metal shoe against a rock broke the morning silence. A tall lean man rode down the trail from the badlands, straddling a stout gray gelding. Gospel Cummings stepped his horse into the trail and spoke sharply.

"Stand your hoss, stranger!" he ordered crisply.

Tod Werner dipped his hand down for the gun in his right holster. Gospel Cummings clicked baek the hammer of the gun in his own big fist. Werner heard the warning and snugged his pistol back in the leather.

"Hold-up, eh?" he muttered. "Well, I'm traveling light when it comes to cash!"

"Frisk this saddle-tramp, Red!" Cummings barked.

Stang rode out of the trail-side brush, circled Werner, and lifted the outlaw's gun from the buscadero holster. Then he slapped Werner for a hide-out pistol, and quickly snatched a leather wallet from Werner's left hip pocket. Gospel Cummings widened his eyes.

"That's Jeff's leather," Cummings growled. "Light down off that gray!" he ordered sternly. "Red, you light down too, and frisk this saddle-tramp to the hide!"

"Lay off," Werner said thickly. "Are you gents the law in these parts?"

"I'll ask the questions," Cummings said gruffly. Red Stang pulled a sack of tobacco from

Werner's shirt pocket. A paper came out with the tobacco, and Stang read it curiously. His nostrils flared as he passed the note to Cummings.

"They're holding Connie for ransom," he said quietly.

Gospel Cummings took the paper and read the note. His eyes narrowed when he stared at Werner. The outlaw shifted uneasily. Red Stang was searching another flat wallet.

"This hombre is Tod Werner," he told Cummings. "Tod Werner belongs to the Stokes gang!"

"The Stokes gang?" Cummings repeated. "You mean that owl-hoot outfit from down Texas way?"

"That's right," Werner admitted. "You do anything to me, and Ben Stokes will kill Dawson and the gal!"

"Making war on women, eh?" Cummings said scathingly. "You owl-hooters ain't Texans, that's shore and certain. Has anything happened to Connie Brighton?"

"Not yet, it ain't," Werner said with a sneering smile. "So you better let me ride about my chores."

Red Stang raised his heavy six-shooter. He was standing behind Tod Werner, and he brought the barrel of his weapon down on Werner's skull. He caught the falling man as Werner crumpled, and Cummings frowned his disapproval. "What's the idea?" he demanded.

"I aim to tie the owl-hooter up, and likewise hobble his jaw," Stang said quietly. "That away we won't be bothered with a prisoner, and he left a plain trail from wherever he came!"

He took a piggin'-string from his saddle and bound Werner's hands behind his back. Another short rope trussed up Werner's ankles, and Stang used the blue bandanna neckerchief around the prisoner's throat to make a gag. Then he pulled Werner from the trail into the heavy bracken. Red Stang mounted his horse after tying the gray to a mesquite bush where the beans hung thick. Stang glanced at Cummings and pointed up the trail with his chin.

"Lead on out, Gospel," he said slowly. "I've taken a liking to my new boss, and looks like he needs some help!"

"Which you won't lose anything by playing it straight with Jeff Dawson," Cummings agreed bluntly. "When Jeff trusts a man, he trusts him all the way, and he don't expect any shady deals!"

Stang glanced at Cummings sharply. The gaunt plainsman was tightening the latigo on old Fred, with his head turned slightly to hear Stang's answer.

"I'll play it square with Jeff," Stang said huskily. "And I'll make it tough on any of those owl-hooters who think they've got away with a sure thing!"

"Being brash won't get us nowhere," Cummings

cautioned. "I know this country back here, and you don't. We'll take it single file up this deer trail!" He started his horse without further explanation.

They followed the spoor left by Werner's horse, and after riding for a mile, Cummings reined his sorrel to a stop.

"This sign is leading to Lost River Cave," he told Stang. "If Stokes has posted a lookout, we won't have a chance to get in that cave."

"I've been around here a spell," Stang answered thoughtfully. "Seems like I heard a yarn about you finding a secret entrance to that cave."

"That's right," Cummings admitted. "But it might not work; Stokes might have heard the yarn too."

"They couldn't have been here long," Stang reasoned. "Let me ride up the front way, and you circle around and try that old trail."

"It's worth a try, but don't take any fool chances riding up to the cave from the front. They could pick you off like a sitting duck on a pond!"

"What's the play?" Stang asked curiously.

"Give me fifteen minutes," Cummings answered. "I'll crawl down through that chimney. I'll wait till I hear you call from the trail down in front of the cave. If we're lucky, I'll take it up from there, and save old Cole that ten thousand dollars!"

Cummings sent his sorrel up a choked deer-trail

to the the right. He climbed a steep path, tied old Fred to a 'squite bush, and proceeded on foot. Five minutes later he stood beside a pile of rocks with his catch-rope in his hand.

Cummings found a stout branch and fitted it in the hondo of his lass-rope. He climbed into the chimney hole, placed the branch across the opening, and lowered himself cautiously. The oily smell of bats filled the sloping tunnel, and there was the danger of scorpions or snakes in the dank darkness. But Gospel Cummings shrugged and lowered himself to the end of the rope.

When his boots touched a rocky shelf, Cummings opened his eyes and turned slowly. He could smell the odor of wood-smoke, and then he saw the glowing coals of a fire not far from his hiding place.

He was on a high shelf about eight feet above the floor of the big cave. After his eyes had become accustomed to the gloom, Gospel Cummings looked around carefully. He sighed gently when he discovered that there was no guard. He could hear movement on the floor of the cave, and he could make out the outlines of a guard at the front entrance to the cave.

He stiffened when he saw Jeff Dawson sitting on the floor about ten yards away, with his back to a limestone pillar. Connie Brighton sat by Dawson's side, her head on the cowboy's shoulder.

Cummings slowly drew his six-shooter. Sitting facing the pair, with his back to the cave entrance, a tall burly man was watching Dawson with a six-shooter cradled in his hand. Cummings raised his pistol and drew a fine bead on that big right hand.

A minute passed, and then Red Stang's voice called from the trail leading up to the cave entrance, "Hello, the cave! I'm coming up, so don't shoot!"

Ben Stokes leaped to his feet like a cat. Jeff jerked erect, and Connie awoke and sat up with a start. As Gospel Cummings watched, Red Stang stepped into view at the entrance to the cave.

Gospel Cummings seized the chance to lower himself to the floor of the cave from the shelf. His pistol covered Stokes, and the outlaw had Red Stang under his cocked six-shooter.

"Don't shoot, Stokes!" Stang said quietly. "Or you will be a dead man!"

Ben Stokes smiled indulgently. "Too much strong drink," he said reprovingly. "Or do you really think you're that fast with your cutter?"

"I'm fast enough, but there are some who are faster," Stang answered.

"Jeff Dawson, mebbe?" Stokes prompted. "Jeff ain't packing his shooting-iron right now."

"I came to talk about Jeff," Stang started again. lie wondered if Gospel Cummings were in position, but he did not want to give the surprise away by venturing a look to the rear.

"Keep on talking," Stokes suggested. "What about Dawson?"

"You tell me," Stang countered. "Why did you take him and the girl?"

"Wanted to have a little talk with him," Stokes answered. "Thought mebbe he could help me in a deal I had in mind."

He hefted the heavy gun in his right hand as he studied Red Stang's face. Stang spoke quietly. "Don't shoot, Stokes!" he warned the outlaw again.

"Yeah? Well, just make a pass for your hardware!" Stokes growled. "How'd you get up here?"

"Followed your trail," Stang answered honestly.

"You're a liar!" Stokes accused him bluntly, "You caught up with Werner, and followed his back-track!"

"I stand corrected," Stang admitted. "Tell him, Gospel!"

Ben Stokes smiled sneeringly. "Try again, sonny," he said with a chuckle. "There's another hombre behind me with a cocked gun at my head, and I'm supposed to turn around and look."

"Drop that gun, Stokes!" Gospel Cummings ordered sternly. "You was right the first time!"

Stokes dropped his gun slowly to the floor. Red filled his own hand as he moved forward. He reached for a hunting knife at the back of his belt, severed the thongs which bound Jeff Dawson, and pushed the gun he had captured from Werner into Dawson's hand.

Jeff Dawson reached behind Connie Brighton and pulled the slip-knot that held the girl's wrists captive by the piggin'-string. "Glad you came, Red," Dawson said gratefully. "Stay where you are, Gospel!" he warned sharply. "There's two more hiding back deep in the cave!"

"Yeah, and drop that hardware!" a hoarse voice shouted promptly. "Or we'll drill the pair of you!"

"Tell 'em to hold their fire, Stokes," Cummings spoke from the darkness. "If they burn powder, I'll get you sure as sin!"

"Don't get trigger-crazy, you two!" Stokes shouted hastily. "There's another one of 'em, and he's got a cutter aimed at my heart!"

"You do the talking," a voice called from the darkness. "We can kill these two jaspers and the gal if that other gent gets brash!"

"She's a draw, the way I see it," Stokes said quietly. "You shoot me, and my pards shoot all three of you. Then they'll get this other jigger back there in the dark. He'll have to come out sometime!"

"We'll make a trade," Gospel Cummings offered. "Dawson and the gal ride out with Red, and I'll take my own chances!"

"You won't get this pair of love-birds," Stokes promised grimly. "Even if you were fairly lucky, you wouldn't get 'em alive!"

"Meaning you'd shoot a woman?" Cummings asked slowly.

"Meaning I think more of my own skin than I do of hers," Stokes retorted. "Want to try me out?"

"I'd like to, with an even break," Cummings answered promptly.

"Keep Dawson and the gal under your guns!" Stokes ordered his two henchmen. "What about that deal you offered me, Dawson?" he asked Jeff.

"You don't have to deal with him, Jeff!" Cummings shouted. "It's even-steven, or I'll get Stokes first!"

"Then my men will get these other three," Stokes said carelessly. "We've lived a long while on borrowed time anyhow. What you say, Dawson?"

"I'll keep my promise," Jeff Dawson answered without hesitation. "That's as far as I'll go!"

"And you'll keep that promise," Stokes said. "You'd make a mighty poor owl-hooter. Name the time and place!"

"Tonight at twelve, at Hunter's Springs," Dawson said quietly. "I'll ride alone, and you do the same!"

"Suits me," Stokes agreed. "There's just one thing. What about Tod Werner?"

"We'll turn him loose when I ride back from the Springs tonight," Dawson offered. "We ain't any part of the law. You and yours will ride out and quit the country!"

"I dropped my gun, but I trust you," Stokes said quietly. "Give me your hand on it, and your pards can ride out without harm!"

"What's this all about, Boss?" Red Stang asked. "What for kind of promise did you make this outlaw ramrod?"

"That's between me and him," Dawson said quietly. "I'm asking you to take orders, Red. It's got to be that way!"

"That's the way it will be," Gospel Cummings interrupted. "I don't know about the deal, but I do know you keep your word."

"He better keep it," Stokes reminded. "Me and my boys won't ever be wanted worse than we are right now. We've got nothing to lose!"

"You are forgetting something," Cummings said slowly. "If you don't keep your word, it might cost you your life!"

"So you worry about that for me," Stokes said with a grin. "The way I hear it, you are your brother's keeper!"

"I know places where men get paid for that job," Cummings answered. "I've got all I can do to look after my own shortcomings!"

"So what brings you up here where you don't have any business?" Stokes asked sourly. "I made a deal with the yearling, and it's between him and me!"

"I never did like highway robbery," Cummings answered. "You forced Jeff to make a deal. He will keep his part of the bargain, and you better hold to yours!"

"What about the law?" Stokes asked.

Jeff Dawson turned to Red Stang. "I'm going to ask you and Gospel not to say anything to the Saint until tomorrow morning," he said quietly. "That goes for you too, Connie."

"I promise," Connie answered quickly.

"That goes for me," the voice of Cummings added.

"That leaves me no choice," Red Stang growled angrily.

"You *bandittos* have until tomorrow morning to make tracks going away!"

"Then mebbe you will take out after us," Ben Stokes said, and he smiled at the tall redhead.

"I might at that," Stang answered with a shrug.

"Mebbe not, after you talk to your boss," Stokes said carelessly. "Bear my regards to Terry Boyd when you see him!"

Red Stang jerked up his head. "What do you mean by that?" he demanded.

"Just what I said," Stokes answered. "You'll earn your pay!"

"He's earned it already," Jeff interrupted. "There's been enough palaver, and I'm getting out of here. I'll see you tonight, Stokes!"

"And be sure you ride alone," Stokes warned. "I'm not in this game to lose, as you might have heard."

"Yeah, I heard," Dawson said quietly. "And after spending three years back in the brakes, I don't aim to lose everything now. Is that clear?"

"Clear as mud," Stokes said carelessly. "Get going before me and my boys change our minds!"

Dawson put an arm around Connie and walked toward the entrance of the cave. Stokes called quietly:

"Your horses are in that little off-set, Dawson. *Hasta la vista.*"

"Till we meet again, at midnight," Dawson answered.

He walked to the off-set and led out the horses. Red Stang backed to the cave entrance, holding his gun on Ben Stokes. After a long moment, he stepped outside and behind a tall rock at the cave entrance. He heard Stokes call impatiently:

"All right, Cummings. Get out of here!"

When he received no answer, Stang smiled and hurried down the trail where he had left his horse. He mounted and joined Dawson and the girl, speaking softly.

"Gospel will join us at the foot of the trail. He went in and out another way!"

They rode down the trail and into the brush. A moment later, Gospel Cummings came down the steep trail sliding old Fred on the sorrel's tail. "Let's put some distance between us and this place," Cummings said, and took the lead at a fast lope. When he drew rein and eased the pace, Stang asked pointedly, "What about this deal you made with Stokes, Boss?"

"He promised to sell his cattle and turn the

money over to Ben Stokes," Connie spoke up quickly.

"You promised that, Jeff?" Gospel Cummings asked slowly.

Jeff Dawson nodded. "Eight thousand dollars," he said quietly. "It's worth it, for what I found out!"

"You don't have to sell your herd, Jeff," Cummings said thoughtfully. "You've got four thousand in the bank!"

"You can't sell the Triangle D herd, Jeff," Red Stang protested. "I'd be out of a job again!"

"I got in a tight, and I took the only way out at the time," Dawson explained simply. "Connie's safety was worth more to me than anything else, and I also found out some things I wanted to know. I figure I made a good deal!"

"What did you find out?" Stang asked curiously.

"I'll talk some other time," Dawson said gruffly. "Right now I've got other things to think about."

"I've been saving my riding pay," Stang said slowly. "I've got something over four thousand. If that will buy say a third interest in the Triangle D, I'd like for to be your pard!"

"Better take him up to keep him honest, Jeff," Gospel Cummings suggested. "You'll save paying him wages, and have a good working hand besides!"

"I got the cash right on me in a money belt," Stang offered eagerly. "What do you say, Jeff?"

Jeff looked at Connie, and the pretty girl nodded emphatically. Dawson smiled then, and stuck out his right hand to Stang.

"Press the flesh, partner," he said softly. "You're a third owner of the Triangle D, starting tomorrow morning!"

CHAPTER TEN

Red Stang rode into the trailside brush, and Gospel Cummings explained to Connie and Dawson about Tod Werner. A moment later, Tod rode out with his wrists still bound behind his back. The neckerchief had been removed from his mouth, and the prisoner was working his jaws and tongue to restore circulation.

"We've got to pass the Circle F," Cummings said slowly. "I'd like to leave Werner there until we turn him loose to quit the country."

"The Saint won't like it none," Dawson said with a grin.

"What the Saint don't know won't hurt his conscience," Cummings said curtly.

The riders made a slight detour and rode into the Box B yard. Old Cole Brighton and his wife came out of the house when they heard the clop of hooves. While Connie was talking to her anxious mother, Gospel Cummings explained to Cole Brighton what had happened. The old cattleman stared at Dawson and held out his hand.

"You'd do that for my gal-chip?" he asked.

"Connie is cow-folks, like I am," Jeff answered quietly. "My Dad always taught me that cow-folks stick together, no matter what."

Cole Brighton's eyes held a faraway look as he stared out toward the badlands. "Some of us might have remembered that when Jim Dawson was accused of something we knew he never did." Then he said angrily, "Let's get up a posse and smoke them killers out!"

Jeff Dawson shook his head. "I made a promise," he said grimly. "I mean to keep my spoken word!"

"Spoken like a man, Jeff," Brighton praised. "Ma and me wants to thank you for taking care of Connie!"

Dawson swallowed noisily and appeared embarrassed. Brighton smiled and gripped the cowboy by the hand. "Let me pay that promise money," he said quietly. "It's the least I can do."

"Thanks, Cole," Dawson found his voice. "But I made a deal, and I'd rather do it my way. I've taken Red Stang in as a third owner, and we'll make an outfit out of the Triangle D before long."

Mrs. Brighton put her arms around Jeff Dawson and kissed him. "Thanks for what you did, son," she whispered. "We won't ever forget!"

Jeff Dawson held the motherly woman close for a moment. Then he broke away and mounted his horse. "I'll see you later, Connie," he called to the girl. "When this thing is settled."

The three men rode to the Circle F with their prisoner. Ace Fleming came outside and stared curiously at Tod Werner. He called to big Charley Bailey and told him to lock Werner up in the supply room.

"The Stokes gang, eh?" Bailey said curiously. "That Ben Stokes is 'Wanted' in a dozen states!"

Jeff Dawson drew Fleming aside. "I'd like to draw four thousand dollars from the bank, Ace," he told the gambler. "I've got to have it right away!"

"Four thousand," Fleming repeated. "Are you going to buy some range bulls to improve your stock?"

Gospel Cummings came over and explained before Dawson could speak.

"To save time, I'll give it to you from my safe in the house," Fleming offered. "The money is in my name at the bank, so we won't have to bother about it. That leaves you about four hundred."

Gospel Cummings jerked his head for Fleming to come to him. "We've got to do something about Terry Boyd," he said in a low voice, when the dapper gambler had joined him. "He brought those owl-hooters in here; paid them with the reward he collected on old Jim Dawson!"

"We'll ride over there tomorrow and have a talk with the Boyds," Fleming suggested. "But first, we better let Jeff finish his deal. It means honor to him, and I'm strong for honor in any yearling!"

Fleming went to the house and returned with the money for Dawson. The three men rode on back to the Triangle D, and once in the comfortable little house, Red Stang pulled off his shirt, removed a money belt, extracted some money from it, and handed the belt to Dawson.

"There's my four thousand, and you better put yours in the belt," he said. "Strap it around your hips for the meeting tonight."

"Thanks, partner," Dawson voiced his gratitude. "Now I'm going to turn in and get me some sleep, if you gents don't mind."

"You do that," Cummings agreed. "I've got to ride down to Three Points and see that everything is all right. Red can do the chores, and I'll be back late this afternoon."

An hour later, Red Stang left the Triangle D on a fresh horse. He rode across the rangeland toward the Box B fence, and went through the motions of riding fence. On his way back, Stang saw a horse-backer loping toward the new panels of the boundary fence. Terry Boyd came up fast on a lean thoroughbred, and Stan waited until the Box B man came to him.

"What's up?" Boyd asked guardedly.

"Hell's a-frying," Stang said curtly. "You brought a passel of Texas owl-hooters up here to the Strip!"

"Says who?" Boyd demanded, and his left eye gleamed balefully.

"The top man," Stang answered. "Gent by the name of Ben Stokes. Ever hear of him?"

"Who hasn't?" Boyd countered. "But he's a liar if he says I sent for him!"

"Says you sent him a thousand dollars," Stang continued. "Anyhow, him and his gang caught Dawson and Connie Brighton last night!"

"They did what?"

"Stokes was holding the girl for a ten thousand dollar ransom," Stang explained.

"You said . . . *was*?" Boyd asked sharply.

Stang nodded. "Like you know, I'm working for the Triangle D, and I fight for the iron that pays my wages. When Jeff didn't show up for breakfast, Gospel and I rode down to look for sign."

"Seems to me you went out of your way to look for trouble," Boyd said sullenly. "After that little talk you and me had back on the Circle F last night."

"That had nothing to do with abusing a girl," Stang replied coldly. "I'd ride against my own brother in a deal like that."

"I'll remember what you said," Terry Boyd growled. "Seems to me like Gospel Cummings gets around a lot."

"Yeah, he always did," Stang agreed. "And he will get around a lot more since he started siding Jeff Dawson. Like I say, me and Gospel rode out there to look for sign."

"So you found it," Boyd filled in. "That old sin-buster is the best tracker in these parts. Well?"

"You wouldn't know much about honor," Stang said pointedly, "but Jeff Dawson passed his word to Stokes. Jeff agreed to sell his cattle and turn the money over to Stokes. He made the deal to save Connie Brighton, and Jeff always keeps his word!"

"Did he raise the money?" Boyd asked.

Stang nodded. "Eight thousand dollars," he answered. "He's riding out to meet Stokes tonight!"

"Stokes is lying when he said I sent for him," Boyd stated flatly. "Where is this meeting to take place?"

"You're not the law," Stang said quietly. "And we promised not to let the Saint know until tomorrow morning!"

"You mean you are going to let Stokes get away with eight thousand in cash?" Boyd asked incredulously.

"Jeff gave his word of honor," Stang explained. "I thought you might want to know, but I'd kill the man who bushed Jeff from the brush. Thought you'd also like to know that!"

"You meaning anything personal?" Boyd asked coldly.

"Yeah," Stang murmured. "You want to make something out of it?"

"Pass it for now," Terry Boyd said. "So why are you telling me?"

"It gives you a chance to show which side you are on," Stang answered quietly. "Jeff can't afford to lose eight thousand right now."

"That's right," Boyd agreed quickly. "If I recovered the money and returned it to Dawson, it would look pretty good to folks in town!"

"Yeah, and like you said, it wouldn't bother your conscience none," Stang agreed. "You say you didn't send for the Stokes gang, and they'd rustle 3 B beef just as soon as any other."

"They wouldn't get far with rustled cattle," Boyd argued. "There ain't enough of them to handle a big drive, and Stokes would know better than to take such a fool chance."

"He wouldn't hardly bother the Circle F," Stang said thoughtfully. "And chances are he would pass up Cole Brighton's Box B." He looked searchingly at Terry Boyd and continued, "But if he had a deal on with somebody on the 3 B, he might run off some of their stock!"

"Meaning anything special?" Boyd asked quietly.

"I was just thinking out loud," Stang answered. "But you might give it some thought."

"I'll do that," Boyd promised. "Now about this promise money. If I could recover that eight thousand for Dawson, it would show where I stand with the Stokes gang!"

"That's how I had it figured," Stang agreed. "Jeff is meeting Stokes at Hunter's Springs at twelve tonight!"

144

"Well, I'll be seeing you around, Red," Boyd said, and turned his horse.

Red Stang watched the 3 B man ride away, and then he turned to ride back to the Triangle D ranch house. He was passing a copse of alders when a drawling voice called to him.

"Ride into the shade, Red. We ought to have a little talk!"

Stang jerked in the saddle when he recognized the voice of Gospel Cummings. The gaunt plainsman stood beside his horse, and his bearded face was grave. He waited for Red Stang to speak.

"I was riding fence," Stang said lamely. "Just happened to meet Terry Boyd, and passed the time of day with him."

"You talked quite a spell with Terry Boyd," Cummings accused him. "Mebbe it ain't none of my business, but he killed your pard's Dad!"

"So you didn't ride down to Three Points," Stang said. "You hid out and then followed me!"

"That's reading sign, Red," Cummings agreed without hesitation. "I wasn't close enough to hear, but you and Terry Boyd had quite a confab. You want to tell me about it?"

"There's nothing to tell," Stang growled. "I was doing the work that had to be done, and I don't like you spying on me!"

"So why are you getting your hackles up?" Cummings asked. "If everything is aboveboard, what do you care who spies on you?"

"Matter of principle," Stang answered angrily. "I used to work for the Boyds, and he was just riding by!"

"And he rides by while your pard is sleeping," Cummings reminded. "Jeff Dawson trusts you, cowboy!"

"I'd go to eternity in my bare feet for Jeff!" Stang declared fiercely. "They called him the 'Lobo Whelp,' but he lived it down, and is trying to make good!"

"So what's all that to you? "Cummings wanted to know.

"Nothing much I can talk about right now," Stang muttered. "What do you aim to do about it?"

"That depends," Cummings said thoughtfully. "You can't play both ends agin the middle up here, Red!"

"I'm playing it straight, Gospel," Stang said earnestly.

"Uh, uh," Cummings contradicted. "Now you take last night at the dance. I had a frawg in my throat. I left the house and went to my horse on account of I had some cough medicine in my saddle-bags."

Red Stang leaned forward, and his face flushed with guilt. "So what-all did you see from back there in the shadows?" he asked defensively. "It must have been something that put you to watching me!"

"That's right," Cummings agreed. "Want to talk now?"

Red Stang drew a deep breath. "So you saw Terry Boyd ride up to the rail," he muttered. "He didn't stay long!"

"No man can serve two masters," Cummings quoted sternly. "Last night I was close enough to hear everything you and Terry said!"

"And you told Jeff to hire me?" Stang whispered. "Why?"

"That way we could watch you," Cummings explained.

"Why do you think I bought in on Triangle D?" Stang asked.

The face of Gospel Cummings hardened. "I could think of several reasons," he answered. "Jeff has no kin, and you just might get the rest of the Triangle D if anything happened to him. You might even get your share of that eight thousand back. And then, there's the outlaw loot hidden some place on the Triangle D!"

Red Stang swore angrily and made a pass for his holstered gun. The right hand of Gospel Cummings swiveled sidewise and came out ready for war. His heavy forty-five six-shooter was eared back and ready to go before Stang's pistol had cleared leather.

"I could have killed you for that fool move," Cummings said quietly, but his deep voice was harsh with an anger he could not control. "Now you stand hitched until I remove temptation from your hand . . . and from mine!"

He stepped around Stang and emptied the cowboy's holster. Red Stang turned slowly and glared at Cummings.

"So now you can tell Jeff," Stang growled.

"If I did, what do you think would happen?" Cummings asked.

"I reckon I'd get killed," Stang admitted readily. "On account of I wouldn't draw agin him, and he'd be blind mad!"

"That's reading the sign," Cummings praised mildly. "So it looks like there wouldn't be any point in telling him right now. I'm trying to make some sense out of your actions, and up to now I don't find any answer that suits me. You want to help any?"

"I didn't do anything sneaky—that is, I mean, not to hurt Jeff," Stang stammered.

"Mebbe not," Cummings answered. "You just might have a reason for what you did, and I'd like to know."

"I can't talk now," Stang muttered. "All I can say is that you ain't helping Jeff any with this pious stuff!"

"You're helping Jeff?" Cummings asked. "By tipping off his enemy about Jeff's plans?"

"That's right," Stang insisted.

"Let's read sign on this play," Cummings suggested quietly. "Jeff rides out there tonight to keep his word to an outlaw we both know has no idea of honor. You send Terry Boyd out to take that money away from Stokes. One of them is bound to get killed!"

"That's right," Stang agreed quietly.

Gospel Cummings stared at the younger man's face. He wanted to like what he saw, but the evidence was all against Red Stang. Cummings finally shook his head and spoke sternly.

"I'm going to turn you over to the law for aiding and abetting a felony!" he said harshly. "I've no alternative!"

Red Stang stared at the bearded face, glanced at the gun in Cummings' hand, and shifted his feet. Cummings warned him, "Jump me, and I'll clip your wings!"

Red Stang turned his back and sat down on a fallen log. His red head drooped dejectedly, and Cummings watched with a bewildered expression in his brown eyes.

"I'll talk, Gospel," Stang whispered at last. "I'll talk if I have your word of honor not to repeat what I tell you!"

"If it's compounding another felony, don't tell me," Cummings warned. "I'll turn you over to Saint John without turning a hair!"

"Sometimes there ain't much difference between the law and an outlaw," Stang said slowly. "I know men who were peace officers one year, and outlaws the next."

"Were you an outlaw, Red?" Cummings asked, but his lips were smiling now.

Red Stang shook his head. "I was a Texas Ranger for two years," he said proudly. "And I earned my pay," he added.

Gospel Cummings nodded his head. "I had that figured," he surprised Stang by saying. "I knew you had ridden behind a law-star."

"How'd you know that?"

"That day you and Shorty Benson jumped Jeff in town," Cummings explained. "You made no move for your six-shooter, but Shorty did. And when Shorty got himself shot up, you didn't do anything about it. Like you might have heard, I can read sign some!"

"I saw Terry Boyd down in Texas," Stang confessed. "I turned in my star and decided to take a little trip."

"Travel broadens a man," Cummings agreed. "You figured you'd been too long in one place, and wondered what was on the other side of the hill."

"Something like that," Stang agreed. "I'd always heard about this Strip country up here in high Arizona."

"Who'd you hear about it from?" Cummings asked bluntly.

"Several fellers," Stang answered. "One was Terry Boyd, the way I just told you."

"Hmm," Cummings mused. "You met Terry Boyd and you wanted to take a trip. You'd ridden behind the law-star."

"Right all three times," Stang answered eagerly.

"So I decided to come on up and see for myself."

"Did it have anything to do with the outlaw loot?" Cummings asked quietly.

Red Stang frowned. "You said you could read sign," he growled.

"So it had something to do with the loot the James gang hid," Cummings continued. "You ain't riding for the law now!" he stated.

"I'm riding on my own," Stang said proudly. "Trying to get me a start, and I mean to settle down!"

"Let's look at it this way," Cummings said slowly. "You used to ride behind a star. John Saint John is what law we have here in the Strip. Seems to me you'd want to help him some!"

"I do," Stang said. "But I want to do it my own way!"

"So far, fair enough, though I don't hold with all your methods," Cummings answered. "Now say Terry Boyd takes that eight thousand away from Ben Stokes. Your next play would be to tip off the Saint so he could arrest Terry Boyd with the goods!"

"The Saint would mess it up!" Stang protested.

Gospel Cummings stared at his younger companion, and a puzzled frown wrinkled his brow. "The Saint is the law in these parts," he murmured. "Mebbe you better talk some more, Red."

"There's other kinds of law," Stang said savagely. "I know where I could get help when I need it!"

"I don't follow you," Cummings said patiently. "I can understand honor, and when a man gives his word. What I can't savvy is all this business of baiting traps for a varmint, when we know both of them fellers is of the same breed!"

"I'll make out a paper and give it to you," Stang offered. "If anything happens to me, Jeff Dawson gets my share. I'll likewise sign off any claim to his share of the Triangle D!"

Gospel Cummings sighed. "I spoke some to Ace Fleming about you, Red," he confessed. "Ace won't do anything unless something happens to me."

"Have you thought it all out yet?" Stang asked quietly. "You going to turn me over to that big deputy?"

Gospel Cummings shook his head. "Uh, uh," he said slowly, and taking Stang's six-shooter he seated it in the tall redhead's holster. "I'm going to trust you, Red," Cummings continued. "A smart feller once said: 'To be trusted is to be saved!' I'm going to let you play out your hand, but I'll be watching you!"

"And you won't say anything to Jeff?"

"I wouldn't dare to," Cummings admitted. "Jeff would ride right over and take it to Terry Boyd before he went to meet Stokes. Jeff lives for nothing but to clear his Dad's name, and to see that justice is done to the man who framed old Jim, and then killed him on a sneak!"

"That's why I'm helping Jeff," Red Stang said quietly, but his young face was like a granite block. "Let's ride back to the spread and get the chores done."

"You ride on, and I'll catch you up," Cummings suggested. "I want to tighten my saddle."

Red Stang climbed his horse and rode away. Gospel Cummings reached to the right tail of his coat.

"Want to say I'm grateful, Gospel," Stang murmured, as Cummings overtook him. "Want to say again that you won't be sorry!"

"I noticed you talking some to Charley Bailey over on the Circle F," Cummings remarked. "Bailey is a good man."

Red Stang turned in the saddle and studied the bearded man's face intently. "Bailey will do to take along," he said quietly. "I was telling him to watch that Tod Werner."

"Heard Charley say one day that you were fast with a cutter, and could call your shots," Cummings said carelessly.

"I'm no creeping snail, but I'd hate to have to face you for a powdersmoke showdown," Stang retorted. "It's a good thing you ain't a killer!"

"Thou shalt not kill!" Cummings said sternly. "I'll stir up a bait of hot grub before we wake the boss, and you throw some hay to the saddle-stock."

CHAPTER ELEVEN

Jeff Dawson leaped from his bunk, clutching at his holster, when Cummings shook him by a shoulder. Cummings spoke softly.

"Let the gun ride, Jeff. It's time for supper."

The meal finished, Red Stang rolled a brown-paper quirly and thumbed a match to flame. He lighted his smoke, inhaled deeply, and glanced at Gospel Cummings.

"I'd like to make that *pasear* with you tonight, Jeff," Cummings suggested thoughtfully. "Just to keep that owl-hooter honest."

Dawson shook his head emphatically. "That would spoil everything," he demurred. "No telling what Ben Stokes would do. This way he'll take the money and leave the country."

"You hope," Cummings said dryly. "Ace will start shoving your Triangle D stock back tomorrow," Cummings changed the subject. "You'll have mebbe sixty head of shipping steers for market."

"We'll have to go slow for a year or so, Red," Dawson said to Stang. "After that we should get along nicely."

"And we can break out that saddle-stock," Stang suggested. "From what I saw, we've got some mighty nice cow-horses."

"And there will be a nice bunch of shippers this

154

time next year," Dawson added enthusiastically. "As we make some money, we can buy a few good range bulls to improve the strain."

"Yeah, it takes money to make money in any business," Cummings said practically. "I hate to see you lose that eight thousand, Jeff." Jeff Dawson frowned. "I wonder how Werner is making out on the Circle F," he said lamely.

Red Stang knew that Dawson was making talk to steer the conversation away from his meeting with the outlaw chief. The tall redhead puffed on his cigarette, and then said he'd wash the dishes.

Dawson and Cummings went to the front room and found seats on the leather couch. Night closed in, and after a while Stang joined the two men. They talked of range conditions and market prices until Dawson stretched to his feet and said he'd be saddling his horse.

Cummings stared at Stang and shook his head slightly. Jeff Dawson went to the barn and lighted a lantern which hung from a rafter near the box stalls. He saddled his horse, slipped the headstall over the delicate ears, and led the horse out to the tie-rail.

Stang watched as Jeff took a thirty-thirty rifle from a set of antlers over the front room mantel. Dawson walked outside and pouched the long gun in the saddle-scabbard under the left fender of his worn saddle. Then he came back to the house, reached for a box of cleaning tools, and started to clean his forty-five six-shooter. This finished to his satisfaction, Dawson washed his hands, nodded at the two men, and settled the brim of his Stetson down over his gray eyes. "I'll see you two gents before breakfast," he said, and left the house.

Stang waited until the thud of hoofs had died away in the outer darkness. Then he glanced at Cummings, who was lounging comfortably in a corner of the leather couch. "What you say if we gear our tops and take a little ride?" Stang asked.

"Later," Cummings answered. "If we ride out there now, Stokes will get ideas. The deal was for them to ride alone."

Out on the trail, Jeff Dawson glanced up at the sky. A sickle moon was just appearing in the east; there wouldn't be too much light. The Triangle D cowboy smiled grimly and patted the stock of his rifle to reassure himself.

Dawson reached the springs just as the sickle moon rode almost directly overhead. A scud of clouds obscured the moon for a time, and Dawson rode behind a stand of timber to study the lay of the land.

"Dawson!" a voice called softly.

Jeff Dawson recognized the rasping voice of Ben Stokes, and his pulses quickened. He waited for a moment until a man rode out from the sheltering rocks. Satisfied that Stokes was alone, Dawson sent his horse forward to meet the outlaw.

"Howdy, Stokes," he greeted the burly outlaw. "I raised the wind like I said!"

"I knew you would," Stokes answered gruffly. "You brought the money with you?"

"I brought it," Dawson answered, and he pulled out the tails of his shirt. He fumbled at the money belt, unfastened the buckles, and passed the belt to Stokes. "It's all there," he said curtly. "If you're smart, you'll ride out tonight!"

Stokes took the belt and looped it around his saddle-horn. "Good luck with your hunting," he said quietly. "And may your hoss never grow lame!"

"Thanks," Dawson said gruffly. *Adios!*

He turned his horse and rode away in the pale moonlight. Ben Stokes watched the broad back and then tucked the money-belt down into a saddle-bag behind his cantle. He dismounted for a moment to tighten the cincha, and then stiffened when a voice spoke behind him.

"Elevate and stand hitched, Stokes!"

Ben Stokes turned his head slowly. A tall slender man was covering him with a heavy rifle. The man wore a bandanna mask on the lower part of his face, but Stokes had recognized the muffled voice.

"What's the idea, Boyd?" he asked quietly.

"The old double-cross," Terry Boyd said thickly. "You told that yearling that I sent for you and your gang!"

"Did he tell you that?" Stokes asked. "I thought you and Dawson were edging at each other on account of your bush-whacking his old man from the brush."

"What did you say?" Boyd asked, his voice a silken purr.

"I said the yearling was on the prod because you killed his father," Stokes answered evenly.

Boyd accepted the amendment. "That's better. Why did you tell Dawson that I sent for you to come up here?"

"Which you did!" Stokes said slowly. "I made the best deal I could for myself, and you do the same!"

"I aim to," Boyd said bluntly. "Pass that money belt over before I drill a hole through your back!"

"I never argue with a gun," Stokes said quietly. "But I reckon you know what this means, Boyd!"

"Reckon I do," Boyd sneered. "You won't leave the country, and the law will run you down!"

Ben Stokes took the money belt from his saddle-bag and threw it to Terry Boyd. Boyd caught the belt with his left hand, holding the rifle with his right.

"I'll make you a little bet, Boyd," Stokes said quietly. "I'll bet you my horse against yours that you don't keep that money long!"

"It's always open season on wolves," Boyd stated. "You are wanted two thousand dollars worth, in Texas!"

"This ain't Texas," Stokes said slowly. "And you ain't the law!"

"Add two thousand to this eight, and it makes ten thousand," Boyd counted out loud. "And you won't be in any condition to talk!"

"Meaning what?" the outlaw asked curiously.

"Meaning that dead men tell no tales," Boyd explained.

"I can read your mind, Stokes. You figure you might as well take a fighting chance. You will make a stab for your belt gun, and I'll shoot in self-defense!"

"You are a louse, Boyd," Stokes said quietly. "Now I know what happened to old Dawson. You claimed self-defense that time too. Then you prove yourself a hero by claiming the bounty on his scalp!"

"I hold the high cards up here," Terry Boyd boasted. "You talked too much, but you won't repeat the same mistake again."

"I've been an owl-hooter a long time," Stokes said scornfully. "I've hid in the brakes, and I've broken most of the laws. But, Boyd, you've got any outlaw faded I ever saw. You double-cross your own folks, you let on to be siding the law, you make a deal with me to do your dirty work, and now you steal loot from an outlaw!"

"You all talked out?" Boyd asked.

Stokes drew a deep breath and relaxed. "Thanks for telling me," he said in a hoarse whisper. "Go ahead and murder me, you mangy coyote!"

"How you want it, head or heart?" Boyd tormented the doomed man.

"What difference does it make?" Stokes asked. "It's murder either way, on account of we've got witnesses!"

"Hog-wash!" Boyd sneered. "That one had long white whiskers when I was kicking slats out of my crib!"

"There's two boss-backers not more than a hundred yards away," Stokes said quietly. "Looks like the Boyd boys to me!"

Terry Boyd jerked a quick glance over his shoulder. He recognized his brothers, and spoke jerkily.

"I'm going to give you a chance you don't deserve, Stokes," he whispered. "Jump your saddle and get long gone!"

Ben Stokes was an opportunist. He leaped to his horse without wasting time in thanks or argument. His spurs bit into the flanks of his mount, and the outlaw rocketed away toward the lava badlands.

Terry Boyd lined his sights and pressed the trigger. As the rifle barked, Stokes cut his racing horse sharply to the right. A bullet nicked his left shoulder, and then the outlaw was gone.

Terry Boyd faced his brothers with the smoking rifle in his hands. Tom dismounted and ground-tied his horse.

"What you up to, Terry?" he asked sternly. "Me and Dix have been keeping tabs on you some!"

160

"I was helping the law!" Terry Boyd said brazenly. "That was Ben Stokes, and there's a two-thousand dollar reward on his head!"

"I hate and despise a bounty hunter!" Tom Boyd said scathingly. "Now you listen to me, Terry. You might as well drop that rifle, on account of Dix has you under his gun, and the hammer eared back!"

Terry Boyd jerked a glance at Dixon and snarled angrily as he let his rifle slip to the ground.

"What's the idea of throwing down on me?" he shouted. "Are you taking up for an outlaw?"

"Stop it!" Tom said sternly. "I'm taking that belt you've got looped around your left arm. If he gives me trouble, wing him, Dix!"

"Wing him, nothing! I'll kill him!" Dixon Boyd threatened savagely. "He's done nothing but bring us grief ever since he rode down to Texas!"

"I went down there on business," Terry Boyd said hoarsely. "We needed money for breeding stock, and I know where to get it!"

"Meaning that outlaw loot supposed to be hidden up here?" Tom Boyd asked scathingly.

"We never needed money until you gambled away all the profits of the 3 B," Dixon accused him. "And we don't need outlaw money now. Fill your hand, Tom, in case this wolf gets an idea to jump my gun!"

Tom stepped forward behind his own drawn six-shooter. He snatched the money belt from Terry, and backed away. Then he spoke sternly.

"Now I'm going to give you a chance, Terry. The kind you gave Ben Stokes. Fork your bronc and make tracks going away. If you stay here an hour longer, I'll make a report to the law, and you and Stokes can fight it out on even terms. There will be a price on *your* scalp!"

"You'd turn against your own flesh and blood?" Terry whispered.

"From now on, you ain't any kin to me and Dix," Tom Boyd said sternly. "You don't own any part of the 3 B, and this money goes back to its rightful owner!"

"I'll ride, but I'd like to know," Terry Boyd muttered. "How did you find out about the money?"

"You guess," Tom countered. "There were a lot of people mixed up in this go-around. Cole Brighton knew, also Ace Fleming, not counting Gospel Cummings and Red Stang. You want to kill all them fellers?"

"Red Stang, eh?" Terry Boyd murmured.

"Mebbe you didn't know," Tom Boyd said quietly. "Stang is now a third owner of the Triangle D!"

"Why, the dirty double-crosser!" Terry Boyd ripped out.

"Call yourself names, Terry!" Dixon Boyd told his brother. "Now you climb your saddle and get! Walk with him to where he left his horse, Tom. He makes a funny move, I'll skotch him like any other side-winder!"

Terry Boyd crouched, and for a moment it seemed as though he would make a desperate fight to save something from the wreckage tumbling about him. Then he straightened slowly, raised his hands level with his shoulders, and tried talking again.

"I meant to give that money back to Jeff Dawson," he began, "to help him get a start on his shoe-string spread!"

"You lying hound!" Tom Boyd burst out angrily. "You've been wanting those two sections of land, thinking that outlaw loot is buried there. If Dawson had eight thousand dollars to the good, we all know right well he never would sell that land!"

"I figured him to haul his freight with that much money," Terry muttered. "I figured I owed him that much!"

Dixon spoke grimly. "Anything you owe Dawson, the chances are you will have to pay it!"

"And it won't be money," Tom added. "Money you can give back, but there are other things you can't, and you know what I mean!"

Tom Boyd reached out and took Terry's six-shooter. He opened the loading gate, placed the hammer at half cock, spun the cylinder, and ejected the shells. "Just to keep you honest, Terry," he explained. "I'll take that rifle back with me. Where did you leave your cayuse?"

"Yonder behind that stand of cottonwoods,"

Terry Boyd growled. "I'll square up with you and Dix one of the days!"

"Why don't you change your name?" Tom Boyd suggested. "You ain't no kin of mine any longer, you ring-tailed skunk!"

He saw his brother climb his horse and ride away. Tom Boyd walked back to his own horse and mounted up. He shook his wide shoulders back and spoke curtly to Dixon. "Let's hit out for the Triangle D and get this over."

Dixon Boyd nodded, and they rode across the range through the pale moonlight. A few minutes later they skirted a heavy stand of cottonwoods, and neither man saw a tall horseman who drew his horse back into the deeper shadows.

Gospel Cummings dismounted and held the nose of his horse to prevent a warning whinny. Red Stang was performing a similar office on his Morgan horse, and when the Boyds were out of sight, Stang spoke in a whisper. "What do you reckon, Gospel?" he asked. "This game is getting all mixed up!"

"Looks to me like they are heading for the Triangle D," Cummings answered. "Let's cut across that barranca yonder and see if we can beat them there."

The two men rode into a deep barranca which cut over toward the west. When they emerged from the draw, they kept up the pace. Red Stang glaneed back over his shoulder.

"We're ahead of them," he said thankfully. "I can see big Tom sky-lined back yonder about a half-mile!"

Gospel grunted and raced on. They rode into the Triangle D a few minutes later, stabled the horses, and went on to the house.

Jeff Dawson came out and stared at the two men suspiciously. "Where were you two hombres?" he asked bluntly.

"Just riding around," Cummings answered soothingly. "Did you have any trouble?"

"Nary a bit," Dawson answered tartly. "I get it now. You two rannies tailed me and stayed at a distance. You let me pass you, and then you rode on back home!"

"That's reading sign, Jeff," Cummings admitted. "Just in case Ben Stokes was pulling a double-cross, we meant to keep him honest."

"I didn't need any help," Dawson growled. He cocked his head and walked to the door. "Hoss-backers coming," he said curtly. "Who could that be at this time of night?"

Gospel Cummings walked to the door and scanned the horizon. "Looks like Tom Boyd," he said slowly. "Him and Dix!"

"I don't want no truck with any of them Boyds!" Jeff Dawson said hotly. "They still believe that old Jim stole their payroll!"

"It won't hurt none to talk, and we've got them outnumbered," Cummings reminded. "You ain't riding the owl-hoot trail any longer, Jeff. You've got to learn to be neighborly."

"Any business they had with us could wait till morning," Dawson argued. "Keep your hardware handy just in case they are painted for war!"

"We'll watch them," Cummings promised. "But it might be interesting to hear what Tom has to say."

Dawson growled, but he walked back into the house. The Boyds dismounted and tied up at the rail. Tom Boyd hailed the house in a loud voice.

"Come on in, Tom," Gospel Cummings answered. "What in time are you doing out at this time of night?"

"As if you didn't know," Dixon Boyd said dryly. "We saw you and Stang cut out of that draw and race on ahead." He turned to Jeff Dawson. "Howdy, Dawson," he said civilly.

"Howdy," Dawson grunted. "We don't want none!"

"None what?" Dixon Boyd asked with a frown.

"No truck with the 3 B," Dawson said brusquely.

"Did you lose any money tonight?" Tom Boyd asked pointedly.

Jeff Dawson made a slap for his pistol. Gospel Cummings caught that slapping hand and held the gun in the holster.

"Quit fighting your head, yearling!" Cummings shouted.

166

He jerked away, taking Dawson's gun with him. Big Tom Boyd watched the little scene, and waited for Dawson to speak.

Jeff turned on Stang with a curse. "Now you better talk, you long-jointed redhead!" he said hoarsely. "I rode after you this afternoon when you thought I was sleeping. I saw you through a pair of field glasses. You met Terry Boyd down by the boundary fence. Well?"

Red Stang stared with his mouth open. He glanced at Cummings, who was stroking his brown silky beard.

"Yeah, I saw you too, Gospel," Dawson said bitterly. "Now these 3 B hombres ride up here. I was better off out on the owl-hoot trail in the badlands. At least I had one friend I could trust out there, and now he's dead!"

Red Stang stared at Dawson, trying to find words. Gospel Cummings also seemed confused, and the Boyd brothers waited for some kind of explanation which did not involve them.

"I was trying to work out a puzzle, Jeff," Cummings said lamely. "I had seen more than I understood, and I was trying to find a few answers!"

"I'm through looking for answers!" Dawson said savagely. "I've been listening to peace-talk, and look what it got me. All the friends I trusted are working with my enemies. Good thing I found out in time. Now I'll know what to do, and I aim to do it alone!"

"You can't go it alone, pard," Red Stang pleaded desperately. "The odds are too many!"

"Don't you call me 'pard,' you sneaking whelp!" Dawson shouted angrily. "If I had my gun on me, I'd call you right now!"

"Mebbe you better tell him, Gospel," Red said pleadingly. "Looks like I let out too many coils, and I'm all tangled up in my own rope!"

"Me and Dix is sorry about old Jim," Tom Boyd said softly. "We aimed to take him, I'll admit that. But we had nothing to do with his killing, and you know it better than most!"

"You're sorry!" Dawson said angrily. "You 3 B hombres put old Jim on the outlaw trail. You tried to buy the Triangle D cheap, and we all know why!"

"Uh, uh," Tom Boyd contradicted. "Me and Dix ain't interested in that outlaw loot. That was all Terry's doings, and that's why we rode over here to see you."

Jeff Dawson turned his back, and tried to control his seething anger. He knew the justice of Tom Boyd's statement, Tom and Dixon had been a mile away when Terry had shot old Jim. He shrugged when Gospel Cummings put a big hand on his shoulder.

"Use your head for something else beside a hat-rack," Cummings said sternly. "When an honest man brings you the pipe of peace, you better listen while he makes his talk. The Boyds told you they don't hold with Terry and his ways!"

"I'll listen," Dawson muttered sullenly.

Gospel Cummings smiled. He walked close to Dawson, pouched the captured six-shooter in Jeff's holster, and nodded at Tom Boyd.

"You hear me, Boyd," Dawson warned. "I aim to get square before I die!"

"And we aim to square up with you before somebody dies," Tom Boyd said quietly.

CHAPTER TWELVE

Tom Boyd watched Jeff Dawson turn slowly. Dawson's right hand was hovering about the grips of his gun, but big Tom Boyd smiled and slowly shook his head.

"Not that way, Jeff," the big cattleman said quietly. "I admire your courage, and your sense of honor. You made a deal with an outlaw, and you went through with the deal!"

"None of your business!" Jeff Dawson snarled.

"No, but it turned into my business," Tom Boyd continued. "Dix and I followed our brother Terry tonight. Terry held up Ben Stokes after you left. He took a money belt from Stokes, and he tried to kill that owl-hooter when Stokes made a run on his horse!"

"You say he . . . tried?" Dawson asked quickly.

Tom Boyd nodded. "Stokes got away," he answered. "He might have been nicked, but he made a fast getaway!"

Dawson asked harshly, "Did Terry make a get-away too?"

"We gave him the same chance he gave Stokes, except we didn't burn any powder," Dixon Boyd said quietly. "Might have been better if we had!"

Jeff Dawson listened, and his face changed. He turned to face Red Stang, who refused to meet his gaze. Dawson's young face hardened.

"So that's what you was telling Terry this afternoon," he accused him.

"I don't know about that part of it," Tom interrupted. "I said me and Dix was going to square up with you. We took that money away from Terry at the point of a gun, so we brought it back to you!"

The change that swept over young Jeff Dawson was startling. He had been ready to fight the entire 3 B outfit. He had gone against the counsel of older and wiser heads in keeping his promise to Ben Stokes. He was positive that he had been betrayed to Terry Boyd by his new partner, Red Stang.

"You brought back the money?" he asked in a husky whisper.

"You can't do business with an outlaw, Jeff," Tom Boyd said vehemently, "no matter what name he goes by. It's your money!"

Tom thrust the money belt into Dawson's hand, and Jeff took it because he didn't know what else to do. He looked down at the belt, glanced at Gospel

Cummings, and then stared hard at Red Stang.

Red Stang was staring at the floor, his face twisted with misery and indecision. Everyone in the room had had a say, but the tall redhead couldn't find the right words.

Jeff Dawson stared at Stang and said, "Well?"

"I feel sick," Stang muttered. "I'm clean as new snow, Jeff. If I take my four thousand, it looks like I'm guilty. I can't get a riding job around here now. I'd have to ride out, and it would look like I was joining Ben Stokes or Terry Boyd!"

"Yeah," Dawson muttered dryly. "And it's not very pleasant back there in the badlands. I ought to know!"

"So?" Stang asked miserably.

"So you get away from me and the Triangle D!" Jeff Dawson said fiercely. He tossed the money belt to Gospel Cummings. "Take my four thousand out and give Stang the belt and his money."

Gospel Cummings took the belt and opened a flap. He counted out paper money while the rest watched silently. Cummings handed the belt to Red Stang, and passed the other money to Dawson.

"Where are you going, Red?" Cummings asked quietly.

Stang shrugged his left shoulder dejectedly. "I'll sleep with the owls," he said bitterly. "Looks like I played my cards all wrong."

"Looks like you didn't have any control over

circumstances, Red. Not any more than Jim Dawson and Jeff had when the 3 B payroll was stolen."

"That made me the Lobo's whelp," Jeff Dawson said sullenly.

"Dix and I are sorry about that," Tom Boyd spoke up earnestly. "We know now that old Jim never did that job. That scheme was hatched out closer to home," he said honestly.

"I might as well tell you, Tom Boyd," Dawson said quietly. "Terry killed my Dad on a sneak, and I took an earnest to square up for old Jim!"

"Know how you feel, Jeff," big Tom Boyd murmured. "It's between you and Terry. Be careful; he's tricky as a coon!"

"I learned some things from Stokes while I was back in Lost River Cave," Dawson said quietly. "I got the proof that old Jim was honest, which I knew all along. Now I know I'm right, and it will help me keep my promises and pay off my debts!"

He glanced at Red Stang with his lips curling. Stang sighed and drooped his shoulders in dejection.

Gospel Cummings changed the subject quickly. "Ride home and stay around with me for a few days, Red," he said to Stang. "I've an extra bunk, and grub enough for simple living."

"Thanks, Gospel," Stang accepted the invitation gratefully. "It will give me time to untrack my mind."

"Hoss-backer coming," Dixon Boyd said suddenly. "You reckon who that could be?"

Gospel Cummings listened and stroked his silky beard. "The law is riding in, gents," he announced. "That's John Saint John, and don't give your right names!"

Red Stang stared at Cummings, who was watching the door. A horse loped into the yard, slid to a stop by the rail, and heavy boots thudded to the ground. Spurs dragged toward the house, and then Saint John entered the room without knocking.

"I got here in time!" the big deputy said with a sigh. "What you Boyds doing over here, Tom?"

"Trying to right a wrong," Tom answered without hesitation.

"I ought to wrap the jail around you, Jeff!" Saint John barked savagely. "For aiding and abetting a wanted criminal to escape!"

"I helped no criminal to escape," Dawson denied the accusation. "You're whistling past the graveyard!"

"Many a true word spoken in jest!" Saint John agreed. "And that's where you are apt to wind up, taking the law in your own hands!"

"At least I got some action," Dawson answered tartly. "I'd still be back in the tangles if I'd waited for you."

"Don't give me any slack-jaw, cowboy!" the big deputy shouted. "I'm the law in these parts, and you aided and abetted Ben Stokes to quit the country. He's wanted in a dozen states, and you knew it!"

"So you're the law," Dawson retorted. "Take out after him, and good luck to you!"

"Which you'll need it," Cummings added. "You make a big target, Saint. You run too much to 'paw and beller,' but it will take more than noise to run down Ben Stokes and his gang!"

"I can start by wrapping the calabozo around the man who helped him," Saint John threatened.

"I had a hand in it," Red Stang spoke up. "I was pards with Jeff for a time."

"Consider yourself under arrest!" the deputy barked. "Both you and Jeff Dawson!"

"Did anyone sign a complaint?" Gospel Cummings asked slowly.

"Don't need any when a pair of hombres compound a felony," Saint John said triumphantly.

"Look, Saint," Cummings continued. "You don't have any witnesses, and a man does not have to testify against himself. Where does that leave you?"

"Up Coon Creek in a leaky boat, and no oars," Tom Boyd said.

The deputy turned on Boyd furiously. "The same charge goes for you!" he shouted. "You allowed Terry Boyd to commit a hold-up, and you let him ride away!"

"Prove it!" Tom Boyd challenged.

"I can prove it!" Saint John blustered. "I caught Terry Boyd, and he talked!"

"You've got Terry in jail?" Tom Boyd asked slowly. Saint John flushed and lowered his eyes. "I had him in jail, and I'll have him there again!" he asserted.

"You mean he got away?" Cummings asked.

"Pulled a hide-out gun on me," the big deputy admitted viciously. "I'm getting up a posse come daylight!"

"Don't look at me," Cummings told Saint John. "I'm no part of the law!"

"Count me out," Red Stang added. "I'm under suspicion."

"Here's a chance made to order for you, Jeff," Saint John said to Dawson. "Terry Boyd killed old Jim, your Dad!"

"Yeah," Dawson agreed savagely. "That's what I told you when Gospel and me brought old Jim to town. You told me it was always open season on wolves, and it still is!"

Saint John glared at Dawson, and then he exploded violently. "I aim to keep law-and-order in these parts if I have to start right here in town!" he bellowed. "I'll do it by handcuffing you and Stang, and riding the both of you to jail!"

"You won't," Red Stang contradicted quietly. "You can't get us both, and you know it. You better think up something better."

"Don't tell me how to do my law-work!" Saint John shouted. He turned back to Jeff Dawson. "You know the badlands, Jeff," he began quietly. "You have a score to settle. You and I can ride back there and trap that owl-hooter!"

"You said I was under arrest," Dawson told the big deputy. "I wouldn't ride with a law-pack noways!"

"You'll ride if I say so!" Saint John bellowed.

Tom Boyd nodded at his brother and started for the door. "You wouldn't hardly expect me and Dix to ride in your posse now," he said quietly. "We're making tracks back to the 3 B."

"I'll get Terry Boyd!" Saint John promised. "I'll subpoena you two Boyds, and you'll have to tell the truth under oath!"

"We'll be seeing you around," Tom Boyd said, and walked from the room, followed by his brother Dixon.

"We might as well be riding, Red," Cummings said to Stang.

"Stay here on the Triangle D tonight," Dawson suggested. "It's mighty late to be riding, and we can sleep here just as well."

Saint John scratched his square jaw. "I've got a plan," he said slowly. "It's past two o'clock now; it will be light shortly after five. Gospel is the best tracker and sign-reader in the country, and we can pick up the trail at daylight. I'll get some sleep in that big chair yonder."

"Rest yourself, and welcome," Dawson said ungraciously. "But count me out of your posse."

"You'll ride if I say so!" Saint John blustered.

"You said so before," Dawson answered calmly.

"You never learn, do you, Saint?" Cummings asked wearily. "For years you've been a-pawing and a-bellering every time you wanted a posse. You get all hands riled up at you, but you just never learn!"

Saint John flushed and shook his head. "It's made to order," he muttered. "Jeff was back there in the badlands for three years. Terry Boyd killed his old man. You, Gospel; you know every canyon and draw back there in the lavas. Stang has been a Texas Ranger!"

Jeff Dawson turned quickly. He stared at Red Stang, who stared back defiantly.

"You never told me you rode behind a law-star," Dawson said slowly. "I'm beginning to understand some things now!"

"Such as what?" Stang demanded.

"Such as you throwing in with Terry Boyd," Jeff answered quietly. "It all fits into a pattern. The James boys were run out of Texas and Oklahoma. They came up here and buried some loot. You shuck your law-star and ride up here. You make a deal with Terry Boyd who has been hunting for that loot!"

Red Stang made no answer. Gospel Cummings smiled and adroitly confused the issue. "Shorty

Benson rode in here with Red," he reminded. "And we all know that Shorty was no part of the law!"

"A man can be a peace-officer in one state and an outlaw in another," Dawson said dryly. "Remember, Red?"

"You mean Stang might have throwed in with outlaws?" Saint John asked suspiciously. "You mean he saw a chance to make a quick stake if he helped find that outlaw loot?"

Gospel Cummings appeared thoughtful. He too was putting some pieces of the puzzle into place. He remembered the conversation he had overheard between Red Stang and Terry Boyd at the Circle F dance.

"That wasn't the reason I quit the Rangers," Stang said slowly.

"What was the reason?" Saint John demanded.

"None of your business!"

"I'm making it my business!" the deputy said angrily. "I can write to Austin and get your record!"

"It's a free country, and you're the law," Stang answered.

Gospel stared thoughtfully at the deputy and made a suggestion.

"Being the law, you're wasting your time here, Saint. Seems to me you'd ride over to the 3 B and watch for Terry Boyd. He's bound to go back there for supplies, or mebbe a bed-roll."

Saint John tightened his jaw. "Good idea. I'll get right over there after breakfast. You gents can ride along with me!"

Gospel Cummings sighed. He glanced at the two younger men, nodded his head, and sat down to tug off his high-heeled boots.

"I'm going to get some shut-eye," he said heavily. "You jaspers can suit yourselves."

Saint John growled and sat down in a big cowhide chair to pull off his heavy boots.

Jeff Dawson jerked his head at a bunk and looked at Stang. Then he blew down the chimney of the coal-oil lamp, removed his outer garments and boots, and crawled into his bunk.

For several moments Dawson stared into the darkness. He had made a promise to a dead man; had ridden the owl-hoot for three long years. Then there was Connie Brighton. Dawson admitted irritably to himself that he had liked Red Stang. He admired the courage of Saint John, while resenting the big deputy's arrogance. After all, Saint John had made little attempt to capture old Jim and himself when they had been on the dodge.

Personally, Jeff Dawson had little feeling one way or the other about Ben Stokes. The outlaw leader had not used him badly; had kept his trail-wolves from molesting Connie in the Lost River Cave. Dawson sat erect suddenly as a thought struck him.

"Gospel!" he called in a whisper. "Gospel Cummings!"

"Yeah, Jeff," the plainsman answered calmly. "You've been thinking, too?"

"What about Tod Werner? "Dawson whispered. "Charley Bailey was holding him on the Circle F."

"I reckon he's still holding him," Cummings answered. "We never did ride over to give him the word."

"What about Tod Werner?" Saint John asked sharply.

"Nothing, except he's an outlaw," Cummings drawled.

"I should have taken him away from the Circle F," Saint John said triumphantly. "I didn't make any deal with him!"

"But we did," Cummings murmured. "And I've got an idea that you'd have had quite a chore taking him away from Charley Bailey and Ace Fleming."

"Werner will keep," Saint John said sleepily. "I'll pick him up when I want him!"

Red Stang got to his feet and flicked a match to flame with his thumbnail. "Looks like a man won't get any sleep on this spread tonight. I'm going to start breakfast!"

"Call me when it's ready," Saint John grunted, and turned his back to the light.

He was soon snoring loudly, and Cummings pulled on his worn gray pants. Jeff Dawson dressed and stomped into his scuffed boots. He jerked his head toward the kitchen door and went outside.

Gospel Cummings came out and said, "Well, Jeff?"

"Let's get shut of the Saint," Dawson whispered. "I've been thinking—putting one and two together."

"You get the answer?"

"I think so," Dawson whispered. "I'm sure enough to take a chance. After the law rides off, the three of us can take a little ride on our own."

"You including Red?"

"That's right," Dawson answered. "I'm not sure what it is, but Red has a score of his own to settle. It has something to do with that buried loot, and leastways we can watch him. What do you think?"

"You've been reading my mind, Jeff," Cummings answered promptly. "Red had some definite purpose in coming up here, and I'm curious."

"Yeah, I've got a reason," a voice said harshly, and Red Stang stepped from the kitchen door.

"I know part of the reason," Dawson said quietly.

"Name it!" Stang challenged swiftly.

"You might not like it if I do," Dawson warned coldly. "I didn't like it too much myself!"

"Quit clouding the sign," Stang came back angrily. "Bring it out in the open where we can all get a good look at it!"

"You bring it out," Dawson suggested. "It concerns you more than it does anyone else!"

Gospel Cummings gripped each of the younger men by an arm. "Bridle your jaws," he whispered hoarsely. "The Saint is awake, and he's listening. You don't hear him snoring any more!"

"Ears like a bat!" Dawson muttered. "I hadn't noticed."

"Pass it till the law rides on," Stang whispered. "A cowboy can make up his sleep in the winter."

"What's the palaver about?" a loud voice asked crossly. "And the coffee-pot is boiling all over the stove!"

Gospel Cummings rushed back into the kitchen and salvaged the blackened pot. He muttered to express his disgust, dumped the grounds into a trash pile, and said he'd get breakfast.

John Saint John pulled on his britches and stomped into his boots. He glared suspiciously at Cummings, who ignored him.

"I'd like to know," the deputy said sullenly, "what was all the whispering about?"

"None of your business; that's why we were whispering," Cummings answered testily. "No one could sleep with you snoring like a sawmill, so we decided to make some coffee and sit out your nap!"

"My snoring didn't bother me, but that talk behind my back did!" the deputy snarled.

"Do you remember the time you were shot up,

and came down to Three Points to impose on my hospitality?" Cummings asked pointedly.

"That was the first and last time," Saint John answered grouchily. "Begrudging an old friend a place to rest, and a few crusts of bread. You got an extra drink to brace a man up?"

"Look, Saint," Cummings answered sharply. "They sell this stuff at the casino in Vaca town." He passed over the nearly empty bottle grudgingly.

Saint John took the bottle and emptied it, as Cummings knew he would. "Builds a man up where he's all tore down," the deputy said with satisfaction. "That Three Daisies ain't bad medicine."

"You going to retire soon?" Cummings asked.

"No; why do you ask?" Saint John barked.

"Thought mebbe you was saving your money against your old age," Cummings answered sarcastically.

"Well, you know how it is, Gospel," the deputy said defensively. "Being the law, I can't carry whiskey around with me."

"Yeah, and it's expensive too," Cummings added dryly.

"What's this about Tod Werner?" Saint John asked curiously.

Gospel Cummings turned his head to hide the smile of satisfaction which wreathed his bearded face. "Werner is one of the Stokes gang," he answered. "Bailey was to turn Werner loose after Jeff paid that money over to Ben Stokes!"

"That changes my plans some," Saint John said with a smile. "A bird in the hand is worth two in the brush. I'll ride over to the Circle F and put the bracelets on Werner!"

Gospel Cummings turned, and he tried to express chagrin. "Talking with my big mouth wide open!" he muttered. "You said you was going to the 3 B!"

CHAPTER THIRTEEN

Saint John was the last to finish breakfast. He wiped his walrus moustache with a big hand, wiped that hand on the seams of his pants, and twitched his six-shooter free from hang.

"We'll saddle our broncs and ride to the Circle F," he said in his usual domineering tone.

"Correction," Gospel Cummings said bluntly. "The law will ride to the Circle F by his lonesome. You'll find me and Red down at Three Points if you want us. Jeff will be busy here."

"There will come a day," Saint John promised ominously. "A day when you law dodgers will need a mite of help."

"So when that day comes, us law dodgers will help each other, like we always do," Gospel Cummings answered dryly. "Don't let us keep you."

Jeff Dawson had little to say. He avoided looking directly at Red Stang, and the lanky redhead seemed strangely subdued. Saint John saddled his horse and rode away, and Cummings nodded at Stang and went out to the barn.

Cummings and Stang rode out from the barn and called to Jeff. "Be seeing you around, Jeff," Cummings said casually. "You need any help, just whistle for me and Red."

"And I'll come on a fast hoss, Jeff," Red Stang said huskily.

"Thanks," Dawson muttered, and watched the two men ride away. Now he was alone on the Triangle D, and he suddenly missed old Jim. After a few minutes he went to saddle his horse. Something was drawing him to the Circle F, and five minutes later he rode out of the yard at a fast lope.

Dawson rode into the Circle F yard an hour later. He saw Saint John's big horse tied at the rail, and then the deputy came out of the tack room with Charley Bailey. Saint John was evidently angry, and the big Circle F cowboy was in no better mood.

"You should have watched him close!" Saint John was saying. "You were assigned to guard Werner, but you make up your sleep!"

"Take a half-hitch in that loose jaw of yours!" Bailey answered sullenly. "I take my orders from Ace Fleming, and he told me to lock Werner up and then hit my bunk!"

Both men saw Jeff Dawson ride to the rail and

dismount. Saint John bellowed across the yard for Jeff to come a-running, but Dawson squared his jaw and took his time.

"What's all the paw-and-beller about?" Dawson asked the deputy.

"Tod Werner was killed during the night," Saint John growled. "Somebody prised the lock off the tack room door, and sank a knife into that owl-hooter up to the hilt!"

Jeff Dawson knew now why he had felt the strong pull to ride to the Circle F. He watched Charley Bailey's face while he digested the news, and turned his glance on Saint John. True to his nature, the big deputy had antagonized the man he would want most to help him.

"What brought you over here?" Saint John barked at Dawson.

"A hunch," Jeff answered quietly. "You might say I was responsible for catching Werner, and he was promised he would be turned loose to ride out of the country."

"After this don't go about making deals with outlaws!"

Dawson ignored the law. He turned to Charley Bailey and asked, "He leave any sign, this killer?"

"Yeah," Bailey answered. "He left the knife in Werner's heart. You ever see it before?"

Jeff Dawson stepped into the tack room. Tod Werner was lying on his back in a pool of dried blood. A bone-handled hunting knife could be seen in the outlaw's left breast. Dawson caught his breath.

"That's Ben Stokes' knife," he said positively. "I saw it at the back of his belt when he was holding Connie and me back in Lost River Cave!"

"So that puts the blame on Stokes," Saint John said, and his big right hand went down to fondle his six-shooter.

"Not necessarily," Charley Bailey contradicted the big deputy. "Somebody could have taken Stokes' knife, to frame him."

Saint John turned slowly on Bailey. "Are you holding up for Stokes," he demanded sternly.

"I'm reading sign the way I see it," Bailey maintained stoutly. "Don't forget that old Jim Dawson hid out for three years for something he never did!"

Ace Fleming came from the big house and joined the three men. The little gambler listened for a moment, and then spoke to Saint John.

"Better take the body back to town, Saint," he suggested. "We'll help you to tie Werner to his horse, and you'll want to report to the coroner!"

"I'll give the orders on law business," Saint John said angrily. "If Bailey had watched this hombre, he'd be alive now!"

"When did you first hear about Werner being here?" Fleming asked carelessly.

"Last night, on the Triangle D," Saint John answered acidly.

"Why didn't you ride over and get him?" Fleming asked.

"Dead of night," the deputy made his excuse.

"So you made up your sleep first," Charley Bailey accused. "You make a fine figurehead for the law in these parts!"

"Are you telling me how to do my work?"

"Yeah," Bailey answered, and his face was hard. "You want to make something out of it?"

"That will do, Charley," Fleming interrupted. "I'll give the orders on the Circle F, and pay no mind to the Saint. Bring up Werner's horse, and we'll give the law that much of a hand."

"I'd like to deputize a posse among your crew," Saint John said arrogantly. "To ride down Ben Stokes!"

Ace Fleming shook his head stubbornly. "Get up a posse in town," he suggested. "My boys work for me; they'd have signed up with the law if they wanted to hunt down killers!"

"Howdy, Ace," Jeff Dawson greeted the Circle F owner. "Might as well tell you now. I fell out with Red Stang last night."

He briefly sketched the happenings of the previous night, and Fleming listened attentively. Charley Bailey also listened in, and Saint John flushed with anger and embarrassment.

"Red Stang had no part of that hold-up," Bailey said slowly. "I knew Red down in Texas when he was a Ranger. Square as a die."

"You Texans hang together, don't you?" Saint John asked with heavy sarcasm.

Charley Bailey flushed and knotted his big fists. "We do, so remember the Alamo," he warned in a quiet voice.

"If you Tehanners like Texas so well, why don't you stay there?" Saint John asked spitefully.

"That's easy," Bailey answered with a smile. "There are too many places where the local law needs help. That answer your question, law-dog?"

"I never asked you for any help," Saint John growled.

"Make up your mind," Ace Fleming said impatiently.

"He tried the same thing over on the Triangle D," Dawson said spitefully. "Naw, the Saint don't need any help!"

"I believe in helping the law, but I don't aim to be ordered around like a cook's swamper," Charley Bailey added sullenly.

"Mebbe you was a Ranger too," Saint John said.

"Mebbe I was!"

"Was you?" the deputy demanded.

"Write Austin and find out for yourself!" Bailey snapped. "For a gent who needs as much help as you do, you take a mighty poor way of getting any of the same!"

"I don't need no help!" Saint John said arrogantly.

"Then take this corpse back to town and start tracking down the killer," Bailey suggested.

He walked away with his head high, dragging his spurs to tell of his anger. Fleming looked at Saint John and smiled.

"Are you happy now, Saint?" he asked.

"I feel all right. Why?"

"Because you never seem to have a good time unless you are riling everyone up you meet," Fleming stated bluntly. "Think it over, Saint. When you change your mind about riding roughshod over the people you want to help you, ride out and see me again!"

Charley Bailey led the dead outlaw's horse to the tack room. He threw the split reins to the ground, and indicated the body with a thrust of his chin.

"There's his horse, all saddled and ready to go," he said grimly. "Put your load on the saddle and make your ties!"

"Head and heels," Saint John grunted, and leaned down to take the dead man's boots.

Charley Bailey turned his back and walked away. "Come back here!" the deputy shouted. "Take him by the shoulders!"

Charley Bailey shrugged and did not turn his head. Neither did he stop walking, and Saint John started after him. Ace Fleming grabbed the big deputy by an arm.

"Better leave Bailey alone," he warned.

"I'll lend you a hand, Saint," Jeff Dawson offered. "I'll take the boots!"

Saint John scowled and took the dead man's shoulders. He tied the dead man to the saddle by ankles and wrists, mounted his horse, and rode out of the yard leading the pack-horse. Fleming turned to Dawson with his brows raised questioningly.

"What do you make of Red Stang?" the gambler asked bluntly.

Dawson recoiled a trifle at the directness of the question. "I haven't quite made up my mind," he answered evasively. "Old Gospel was telling me about an Indian chief who was made a kind of a circuit judge by his tribe. This old redskin said he would never judge one of his fellows until he had walked at least two moons in that brave's moccasins!"

"So?" Fleming prompted.

"It's a queer feeling, Ace," Dawson confessed. "Mebbe I've walked in Red's moccasins, or it might be he could have walked in mine!"

"So you want a little time to make sure about him," Fleming said quietly. "That's a right good idea. Anything I can do to help?"

"Could you spare Charley Bailey today, Ace?" Dawson asked hopefully. "He's older than me, he's a good hand, and I want to run down some sign on that outlaw loot."

"It's fine with me," Fleming answered. "Hey, Charley!"

Bailey came back slowly to the tack room. His

face showed his resentment of Saint John, but the scowl left his face when Fleming spoke.

"Jeff asked if you would ride with him today, Charley," the little gambler began. "He wants to run down a lead on that outlaw loot."

Charley Bailey tried to hide his excitement, and failed. His nostrils flared widely, and an eager expression of anticipation appeared in his wide gray eyes.

"I'll be glad to ride with Jeff, if it's jake with you, Boss," he told Fleming. "I've heard about the James boys and their treasure, and I'd like to know if any of it is true."

"Saddle your tops and ride on out," Fleming said quietly. "Stay with Jeff as long as he wants your help."

The two men rode out of the yard and quartered toward the east. Charley Bailey was taller than Dawson, six-feet-two, and weighed close to two hundred pounds. He appeared to be about twenty-five, but he had that maturity which comes early to men who spend their lives in the saddle.

"What's on your mind, Jeff?" Bailey asked carelessly.

"I'm mixed up, Charley," Dawson admitted. "I like Red Stang, but I can't rightly figure where he fits in."

"Off-hand, I'd say Red was trying to figure out that same problem," Bailey answered thoughtfully.

"There's something similar between you and Red," Dawson spoke slowly. "I can't quite place it, but it's there!"

"Once a cowboy, always a cowboy," Bailey said with a smile. Red is a mighty good cowhand."

"He's more than just a cowhand," Dawson argued. "He's also a Texan, but there's still a difference I can't figure!"

"He was a law-dog," Bailey said quietly. "He will always think like a peace officer."

"He had a deal with Terry Boyd," Dawson said flatly. "He was playing both ends against the middle!"

"I'd say Red was a square-shooter," Bailey said thoughtfully. "Funny thing down in Texas, say twenty years ago, Jeff. There was sometimes very little difference between a lawman and an outlaw. Fact is, he might have been an officer in Texas and 'Wanted' up in Kansas or in the Nations."

"You mean Red might have been on the dodge?" Dawson asked.

"Down Texas way, you don't ask a man too many personal questions," Bailey answered slowly. "As far as that goes, would that matter to you?"

"I'd give it a lot of thought," Dawson admitted honestly.

"After being on the dodge three years yourself?" Bailey asked pointedly.

"I see what you mean," Dawson admitted. "But I'm sure that Stang told Terry Boyd about my meeting with Ben Stokes!"

"If he did, he must have had some reason," Bailey murmured. "Where we riding?"

"There's a pair of low hills back near the lavas on Triangle D range," Dawson explained. "I know there was a cave there, and it was covered up by a slide. It's one of the few places Terry Boyd didn't look, and I'm curious."

They were now on Triangle D range, and Dawson pointed the lead toward a pair of jutting ridges in the low foothills. The hooves of the two horses made little noise in the thick bunch grass, and they entered a long grassy draw in single file. Jeff Dawson reined to a stop suddenly as he held up his left hand.

"Somebody up ahead!" he whispered tensely. "I saw a Stetson top that hog-back yonder!"

"We better leave the horses here and press on the rest of the way afoot," Bailey whispered. "You any idea who it might be?"

"Could be Terry Boyd," Dawson answered through clenched teeth.

Charley Bailey caught Dawson by the arm. "If it is, don't go to fighting your head like a green yearling!" he warned. "If we are going to learn anything about this puzzle, we want to listen a lot, and keep our own mouths shut. You understand, Jeff?"

Jeff Dawson was folding the grips of his gun.

His breath was coming fast, but he grew quiet under the restraining influence of his older companion. He nodded his curly head.

Bailey now took the lead, and the two men crept through the barranca without making any sound. Five minutes later, Bailey stopped and raised a hand for increased caution. A horse was tethered to a 'squite bush, and both men recognized the 3 B brand on the left hip.

They crouched low and made their way to a stand of creosote bushes which blocked the far entrance to the draw. Both men froze to immobility when they saw another man about fifty feet away, his back to them.

"Terry Boyd!" Dawson whispered softly.

Boyd was also crouching behind a bushy cover, and he was evidently watching someone else. The sounds of digging became perceptible, and Boyd straightened up with a six-shooter in his right hand. He stepped forward into the clear, his voice giving the stick-up command. "Stand hitched and sky them dew-claws!"

Charley Bailey scudded across the clearing like a frightened rabbit, with Dawson at his heels. They stopped behind the cover vacated by Terry Boyd.

Boyd had the drop on a tall burly man who had obediently raised both hands above his head. His face was covered with a stubble of beard, but Dawson recognized him instantly.

"That's Ben Stokes," he whispered almost soundlessly. "He didn't quit the country!"

"Howdy, Boyd," the outlaw leader greeted Terry Boyd quietly, and with no excitement audible in his deep voice. "I heard the Saint had wrapped the calabozo around you."

"Mebbe you had something to do with me going to jail," Boyd said nastily. "What you looking for back here?"

"Treasure," Stokes answered with no attempt at evasion. "Old Fred Haney said he helped plant the loot, and Haney wasn't given to stretching the truth like you and me!"

"Speak for yourself, you owl-hooter!" Boyd said savagely. "You told Dawson I had sent you a thousand to come up here!"

"I told the truth that time," Stokes said with a grin.

"Pass that for now," Boyd growled. "You find anything here?"

"A trace, you might say," Stokes answered. "But it's a job for black powder. You want to pard with me again?"

"Why should I?" Boyd asked.

"We're both straddling the owl-hoot now," Stokes reminded him.

"So it's dog eat dog," Boyd replied. "Where you want it, head or heart?"

"You mean you'd stand there with yore cutter in your hand, eared back to go, and shoot me down like a dog?" Stokes asked.

"Like a lobo," Boyd corrected him. "You double-crossed me once, and you won't get another chance!"

"I should have quit when I was ahead," Stokes said glumly. "Tell you what, Boyd. You stuck me up the other night and took my traveling stake. Not that it did you any good; your brothers trimmed your horns down to the nubs. You holding anything?"

"Sixes full," Boyd answered promptly. "Is that good enough?"

"Uh, uh," Stokes said quietly. "You tried to kill me after giving me the sign to high-tail. You holding any cash?"

"I got three thousand rat-holed away," Boyd admitted. "Keep on talking!"

"I got two thousand," Stokes said slowly. "Not on me," he added quickly. "I'll ante that two thousand for the chance to match cutters with you, winner take all!"

"How long will it take you to dig it up?" Boyd asked curiously.

"I could be back in an hour," Stokes answered. "You?"

"That's time enough for me," Boyd grunted. "I've got you faded!"

Charley Bailey touched Dawson's arm and began a retreat. They reached their horses and rode up another draw, and Jeff Dawson showed his bewilderment.

"When they get the money, we'll step in and take them both for the law," Bailey whispered.

"They'll cross each other up," Dawson argued.

Charley Bailey shook his head. "This thing is bigger than money; bigger than life to either one of them," he explained. "It's what you might call killer's pride. Each thinks he is faster with his tools than the other. This one they will play above the board!"

CHAPTER FOURTEEN

Red Stang stopped his horse on the trailforks leading to the Circle F on the east, to Three Points on the south. Gospel Cummings watched the tall redhead, but he made no comment. Stang finally spoke.

"I'm riding out a ways, Gospel, just to have a look-see."

"I'll ride along," Cummings answered. "Do you mind?"

"I was hoping you'd come," Stang admitted. "There's a place back on Triangle D range I've been looking over."

"You're thinking about that outlaw loot," Cummings guessed shrewdly. "I'll bet it's a spot between two low hills."

"How'd you know?"

Cummings smiled. "The loot is buried between two hills," he said quietly. "Why are you so interested in that old treasure?"

"Who isn't?" Stang countered. "Right now that loot belongs in the Public Domain. It will belong to whoever finds it!"

"Not if it is on private property," Cummings argued. "And the Triangle D belongs to Jeff Dawson. It would belong to the law," Cummings corrected him. "The finder would be entitled to a certain percentage for recovery. Then it would be up to the law to find out just who was entitled to what was left."

"I hear there are a lot of jewels," Stang added. "After all those years, they'd have a hard time proving ownership, seeing that the mountings would be missing!"

"The finder would get a portion," Cummings insisted. "That is, if he turned it over to the authorities."

"I'd like to see Jeff get it," Stang said earnestly. "He deserves something for the misery they dealt him and his Dad!"

"Where do you fit in?" Cummings persisted.

"I'd like to see Terry Boyd get his needings," Stang muttered.

"He do something to you?" Cummings asked slowly.

"Yeah!" Stang growled. "He did something to me!"

Gospel Cummings sighed. He knew cowboys and their moods, their code of ethics, and their stubbornness. Red Stang had said all he intended to say, and what he had said was worth some thinking about.

"Let's ride then," Cummings suggested. "Looks like no one in these parts will get any rest until that treasure is found."

Five miles and forty minutes later, Gospel Cummings reined his sorrel into the brush, followed closely by Stang. Cummings was staring thoughtfully across a grassy swale where a little hillock gave promise of cover. His brown eyes narrowed for better focus. Something had moved up ahead, and the gaunt plainsman watched intently to verify his suspicions. Finally he spoke softly to his companion.

"Easy now," he warned Stang. "I don't know what for, but Jeff is behind that little hill!"

He rode his horse deeper into the brush when the clop of hooves warned of an approaching rider. Red Stang made a little slap for his belt-gun when Terry Boyd rode up the trail at a trot, and Cummings reached out and gripped the cowboy's right arm.

"Hold it, you young firebrand!" Cummings whispered sternly. "Jeff is watching Boyd for some reason, and Jeff isn't alone."

They waited until Boyd was out of sight, and Cummings again took the lead and rode back to the trail. He met Charley Bailey, who showed surprise and disappointment at the meeting, but Jeff Dawson greeted Cummings cordially.

"All we need now is the Saint," Bailey said with a grim smile. "Boyd and Stokes have a meeting for a powder-smoke showdown, and the law could take the winner!" Bailey explained his remarks, and Cummings stroked his silky beard. Dawson and Stang looked each other over doubtfully; neither spoke to the other.

"Them two will talk some more," Bailey said confidently. "We can learn a lot by listening."

Cummings said slowly, "Those two will play for keeps!"

"Save the law a lot of time and money," Bailey said with a shrug. "We'll leave the horses and shag ahead on foot."

"Fan out when we get to those two little hills," Cummings suggested. "That will thin any target we make, and we will have them surrounded on three sides."

The horses were tied up in a thicket of mesquite well off the game trail. Charley Bailey took the lead and started through the head-high brush, his pistol in his big right hand. Jeff Dawson followed, with Cummings at his heels. Red Stang was left to bring up the drag, and he was glad that he did not have to face Jeff Dawson.

After a time, Charley Bailey raised a hand for caution. They were now moving slowly through the bunch grass, and Bailey motioned for Dawson and Cummings to fan out, one on either side. Stang went far to the right, and none of the four made a sound as they carefully placed their boots to avoid crackling twigs.

Dawson came to a little hillock surrounded by sage and creosote bush. He hunkered down and peered through the foliage. No one was in the clearing, but Dawson saw the tops of the brush move over to the left. Then he heard Terry Boyd's voice.

"I see where you are holed in, Stokes. Step out like a man!"

Ben Stokes stepped promptly into the clear. His wide shoulders were hunched forward as though he half expected a bush-whack shot. He nodded approval when Terry Boyd also stepped into the open.

"Did you bring your ante?" Boyd asked.

"I brought it," Stokes grunted. "You?"

"Got it on me," Boyd answered. "If you are lucky, you can take it off my dead body!"

"Great minds run in the same channels," Stokes said with a cold smile. "I never did like you none, Boyd. You just ain't what a hand might call honest."

"What do you know about honesty?" Boyd asked dryly. "You've been robbing and killing since before you rubbed the velvet off your horns!"

"Honest robbing," Stokes defended himself. "Everybody and his blind old step-pappy knew I was an outlaw. You tried to play both ends of the game. You let on to be respectable, and you even robbed your own brothers! I've got a surprise for you," Stokes went on. "I found out who those three jaspers were who nearly beat old Fred Haney to death!"

"Mouthy son, ain't you?" Boyd sneered. "That way, you figure to live a little longer?"

"You and me both have lots of time," Stokes said with a shrug. "Just wanted you to know before I drill a hole through your black heart."

"Pretty confident for a man about to die," Boyd said coldly. "What gives you the idea you've got me faded with my tools?"

"I've seen you draw, for one," Stokes answered promptly. "But that ain't the main reason. I've known killers all my life. Honest killers, and the other kind."

"There's only one kind," Boyd argued. "The pot should call the kettle black!"

"There's two kinds," Stokes contradicted. "One kind shoots in self-defense, or at least with an even break. The other just shoots to kill, even if he has to lay back in the brush and shoot his victim in the back. That kind is seldom really rapid with his tools. He just don't have enough confidence in his own abilities!"

Terry Boyd's face blackened with rage. Stokes smiled to show his contempt. "Don't draw now," he warned. "I'd shoot the buttons off your vest before your cutter could clear leather. In case you didn't know, getting mad slows up the muscles!"

Terry Boyd controlled his anger, and the sneer left his bony face. When he was sure of himself again, he returned to the original subject of discussion.

"The three?" Boyd said lazily.

"Tod Werner was one," Stokes answered. "Joe Stevens was another."

"That's two of your own gang," Boyd tallied. "This third hombre—was it Ad Cross, that other owl-hooter who runs in your pack?"

"Uh, uh," Stokes said, with a shake of his head. "This third feller always throws his shots off a mite high. He's the one who shot old Fred!"

Jeff Dawson leaned forward, his nostrils flaring wide. The same man who had shot old Fred Haney had also shot Jim Dawson. Both had lived for several hours after being shot high above the heart.

Dawson drew his six-shooter and lined his sights on Terry Boyd's back, between the shoulders. His finger tightened on the trigger, and then Dawson sighed and lowered his gun. He had promised Charley Bailey to listen.

"So it could have been you who shot Haney," Boyd said nastily, but it was evident that he was disturbed.

"I never throw my shots off," Stokes boasted quietly. "I put my slugs where I call 'em. Give you one more guess, you bush-whacker!"

Jeff Dawson gasped slightly when two hats

appeared above the brush behind Stokes. He recognized Joe Stevens and Ad Cross, and Terry Boyd saw them at the same time.

"You double-crossing side-winder!" he accused Stokes. "You rigged a sure-thing plant on me!"

"That's right," Stokes admitted brazenly. "That's one I learned from you, Boyd. Remember what happened to me over at Hunter's Springs?"

"So we both lost by not sticking together," Boyd pointed out.

"Which suits me just fine, as long as I couldn't have that eight thousand," Stokes agreed quietly. "That ain't the point, Boyd. Now you take it among owl-hooters; a man only gets one chance to double-cross his pards. You've had yours!"

"The code of old Judge Colt!" Boyd sneered. "I figured that was the one thing that could keep you honest!"

"You better stick to something you know more about," Stokes suggested. "After what you did to Haney and Dawson, you should tell it scarey about the gun-fighter's code!"

"Give me a chance," Boyd pleaded. "I need a traveling stake!"

"Me and the boys have to quit the country," Stokes said carelessly. "You sent for us this second time, and now you talk about playing it square. Shake him down, Joe!"

Joe Stevens came forward behind his drawn six-shooter. He was tall and thin, with a long bony face. "Make one move!" he dared Boyd. "I'll do what I should have done this morning when I saw you sneaking away from the Circle F tack room!"

Stevens jammed the muzzle of his pistol in Boyd's back, ran his hands over the 3 B man, and pulled out Boyd's shirt-tail. A flat wallet dropped to the ground, and Boyd's face expressed his rage.

"They'll nail you for Werner's death, Stokes!" he shouted. "I left your knife in the body!"

Ben Stokes nodded slowly. "I missed that knife after you robbed me of the eight thousand," he said lightly. "That's why I sent word back to the Saint. Takes a thief to catch a thief, looks like!"

"Blow his brains out, Ben!" Ad Cross said viciously. "Tod Werner didn't amount to much, but he was part of the gang. This sneaking snake killed him, and he ain't fitten to live!"

"Easy; I'll give the orders here," Stokes reproved Cross.

Stokes turned to Joe Stevens, and the outlaw's weathered face was a mask of hatred. Terry Boyd watched like a bird charmed by a snake.

"Tell him who that third feller was, the one who shot old Fred," Stokes said to Stevens.

"He was the one!" Stevens said, and he spat to show his disgust. "That old hold-up might have talked after a while, but that wasn't fast enough for Terry Boyd. Let him have it, Boss!"

Ben Stokes shook his head. "Matter of honor," he said fiercely. "Boyd claims he has me faded on the draw-and-shoot. He's wrong, but I promised him a chance."

Jeff Dawson listened, and his eyes widened. Stokes had every reason to kill Boyd, but now he was talking about a gun-fighter's honor. One of the oldest laws in the old West: the code of old Judge Colt.

"Leave me give the go-ahead," Joe Stevens pleaded softly. "I'll keep to the side and take off my J. B. When I drop that old Stetson, you jaspers start clawing for your irons!"

Jeff Dawson stared through the brush with silent fascination. Joe Stevens walked to the side, halfway between Stokes and Boyd. He took off his shapeless black Stetson, held it at arm's length, and glanced at the two fighters.

Ben Stokes was facing Boyd in the gun-fighter's crouch, with his body half-turned to thin the target he presented. Boyd faced the outlaw squarely, his right shadowing the grips of his forty-five.

"You, Bailey and Dawson!" a booming voice shouted. "Where in time are you hombres?"

Jeff Dawson jerked and half-turned his head. Terry Boyd made a frantic dive into the brush, and Ben Stokes threw a shot at him as he took a step to the side and then legged it into the brush. Stevens and Cross had disappeared, and when Dawson slapped for his gun, the little clearing was empty.

But only for a moment. Red Stang leaped from his hiding place and took after Terry Boyd. Jeff

Dawson followed at a run, and he was just in time to see Terry Boyd jump his horse which had stood ground-tied back in the brush.

Red Stang burst out of the brush and threw a shot at Boyd, who answered with his own gun. Both shots went wild, and then Stang's gun roared again.

Terry Boyd had sunk his spurs into the flanks of his horse after that first shot. He sagged as the horse leaped ahead, and Terry Boyd crashed to the ground and bounced in the deer-trail.

Jeff Dawson stared at Stang and drew his own gun, Red Stang was leaning forward behind his smoking six-shooter, and his lips were snarled back to show his tightly-clenched teeth.

"Hold it, Red!" Dawson shouted. "He's wounded bad!"

"Wounded nothing; he's dead!" Stang growled savagely. "I waited three years to make sure!"

Gospel Cummings came running, followed by Bailey. They stared at Terry Boyd, back to Red Stang, and Cummings shook his head.

"Blast that blundering deputy!" Charley Bailey ground out savagely. "We could have taken those other three, but he had to yell his head off when he found our horses!"

"And us up here on foot," Cummings added. "Is Boyd hurt bad?"

"Naw," Red Stang growled. "He's dead, the sneaking side-winder!"

"You ain't the law!" Cummings said sternly. "You could have throwed off your shot!"

"And him getting away?" Stang muttered. "I didn't savvy what kind of play you and Bailey had in mind, but him and Stokes were getting set to burn powder. I was going to wait and see who won, but the Saint bought chips in the game and spoiled the deal!"

John Saint John came galloping through the brush, his six-shooter in his right hand. "What's going on here?" he bellowed. Then he saw Terry Boyd. "Who shot him?" he demanded.

"I did for him," Red Stang said slowly, and now he was calm. "He was wanted by the law, and he was making his escape. He shot at me first, and I let him have it!"

"But you cowhands wouldn't ride in my posse!" Saint John said furiously.

"That's right," Cummings agreed. "You got here a mite too late, Saint. Ben Stokes, Joe Stevens, and Ad Cross were all here too."

"Let's take after them!" Saint John shouted. "They haven't much of a start!"

"Our horses are back a ways, and that's start enough in these badlands," Cummings said with a cold smile. "Of course, you are mounted, and after all, you're the law in these parts!"

"Get your horses, and we'll trail them," the deputy said more quietly. "You can read sign with the best, Gospel."

"They won't go far," Cummings said with a shrug. He walked over to Boyd and felt for a pulse. He shook his head, and his brown eyes expressed sorrow as he looked reproachfully at Red Stang.

"It didn't call for a killing," he said slowly. "You could have winged him through a shoulder, and knocked him out of the saddle!"

"He had a killing coming!" Stang muttered. "I killed him, and I'm glad for the first time in three years!"

Jeff Dawson listened and watched the tall red-head. In a measure, Dawson felt that he had been cheated. He had made a promise at the graveside of old Jim. Now Terry Boyd had paid the penalty.

"Go run for your hosses, you men!" Saint John urged savagely. "We can clean up this nest of outlaws once and for all!"

No one made a move to obey the towering deputy. Charley Bailey spoke quietly.

"Ben Stokes has the five thousand," he reminded them. "He took that three thousand from Boyd!"

"You mean you saw it?" Saint John shouted. "What in tarnation were you jaspers a-doing?"

"Listening, mostly," Charley Bailey said quietly. "Letting those two unload their minds. Getting evidence, you might say!"

"You get any?" Saint John asked sarcastically.

"Some," Bailey answered. "Terry Boyd

admitted stealing Stokes' knife, and using it to kill Tod Werner with. Boyd meant for you to take after Stokes, so why don't you start on a man-hunt, deputy?"

"That wasn't all," Cummings added. "Joe Stevens confessed that it was him and Cross who beat up old Fred Haney. It was Terry Boyd who shot that old owl-hooter!"

"Well, that part is cleared up," Saint John said importantly. "Like I've always held, all the law has to do is keep on looking for sign."

Charley Bailey stared at the big deputy with amazement in his wide gray eyes. "Well, cut my cinchas," Bailey muttered. "Is this big clumsy-footed ox taking credit for something we figured out?"

"Seems as though," Gospel Cummings answered sadly. "Saint means to be right both ways. He's what you might call an opportunist."

"I'm the duly constituted law in these parts," Saint John corrected him stiffly. "And don't none of you hombres forget it!"

"How could we?" Bailey growled. Then he turned his back and glanced at Jeff Dawson.

Jeff Dawson was staring fixedly at Stang. His lips parted, and then Dawson clamped down on his lower lip. What he had to say could wait.

"We'll take Boyd back to town and send word to his brothers," Cummings murmured. "He's shot squarely through the heart!"

"I told you Red could call 'em," Bailey said slowly. "It was between him and Jeff. One of them was bound to kill Terry Boyd."

"I had first call on him," Red Stang said, and his voice was husky. "You gents don't mind, I'll ride back alone. Got some thinking to do."

"Do your thinking some other time!" Saint John barked. "Right now you are riding with me. Get your horse, and step about fast!"

Red Stang turned slowly and faced the big deputy. His lip curled, and his shoulders trembled with anger. Then he whirled on one heel and stalked through the brush without speaking.

"You never will learn, Saint," Cummings said sadly. "Right now that cowboy would see you in Hades in your bare feet before he'd ride with you. He did the work you get paid to do, but you still straddle a high hoss!"

"I'm the law in these parts!" Saint John bellowed angrily. "I've got the authority to swear in a posse when I need one!"

"You don't seem to have much luck," Charley Bailey said coldly. "Give me a hand with the corpse, Gospel. We'll tie him on his own horse, and the law can take him back to town. Seems that's about all he does lately!"

"You give me any more of your slack-jaw, I'll put you under arrest for obstructing justice!" the deputy threatened Bailey.

"You try it, Big Shorty!" Bailey challenged

coldly. "Now you can do your own work; I'm getting back to my own horse!"

Saint John rubbed his square chin. Charley Bailey walked away, and Jeff Dawson followed the big Circle F cowboy. Gospel Cummings jerked his head at the body.

"Unload, Big Shorty," he said curtly. "You take his head; I'll take his heels!"

"I don't want any of yore jaw, either!" Saint John growled.

Cummings straightened up. "You want it that away, so be it," he said quietly. "Load him on yourself!"

He walked away, leaving the deputy with the dead man. Saint John swore savagely as he bent his knees and lifted the body of Terry Boyd. Boyd was not a heavy man, and the deputy raised the body easily.

Red Stang had disappeared, and Charley Bailey was riding south with Jeff Dawson. Cummings shook his head and pointed his old sorrel toward Three Points. He glanced back over his shoulder. John Saint John was riding out of the brush, leading Terry Boyd's horse by the bridle-reins. There would be two new graves in Hell's Half Acre; one service would answer for both.

Cummings reined in at his cabin and went inside. He smiled when he saw two paper bills on the deal table. Two fifty-dollar bills. A note placed under the money read: "For services to be rendered for two members of the Stokes gang."

Gospel Cummings read, and reached for his bottle. He muttered after taking a generous libation, "So Terry Boyd was part of the gang. I suspected it all along!"

CHAPTER FIFTEEN

Gospel Cummings glanced up when a horse stopped at the tie-rail outside his cabin. He saw Jeff Dawson dismount, and a moment later the Triangle D cowboy came into the house.

"I'm about to stir up a bait of hot grub for supper," Cummings said quietly. "Sit a spell and break bread with me."

"Thanks, old friend," Dawson said wearily.

The light had gone out of his eye, and he looked ten years older than when he had come in from the badlands. Gospel spoke gently.

"Don't take it hard, Jeff," he murmured. "Red saved you from having blood on your hands. You've got to think of Connie, you know."

"But Terry Boyd killed my Dad," Dawson muttered. "I had him under my sights back yonder; I near let him have it. Then I remembered what Bailey had said; I listened."

He glanced about the room, saw the money and note on the table, and leaned forward with excitement showing in his face.

"That note?" he asked sharply. "Who wrote it?"

"Ben Stokes wrote it," Cummings answered. "Why do you ask?"

"The man who wrote this note is the same hombre who left that note in my cabin when you and me first rode over to the Triangle D!"

"Knew it looked familiar," Cummings agreed.

"What do you make of it, Gospel?" Dawson asked.

Gospel Cummings shrugged. "Ben Stokes is an outlaw," he answered. "He's been one for years. He never overlooks a bet. It means he wants that treasure buried back there somewhere on the Triangle D!"

Cummings cut steaks from a slab of beef and set his skillets on the stove. Jeff got to his feet and stared at the entrance to the Devil's Graveyard. He said to Cummings as he left the cabin, "I'll be back in a few minutes. I'm going out there to talk with old Jim."

Cummings made no answer, but watched the tall cowboy go through the entrance of the burying ground. Dawson walked between the rows of volcanic headstones. His eyes narrowed when he saw a horse ground-tied at the far end of the cemetery. A Morgan horse with black points.

Dawson clenched his teeth and started toward the horse.

Another mourner was in the place of rest; a tall redhead with a smoke-grimed gun in his holster.

He was kneeling beside an old grave in an attitude of prayer.

Dawson stopped and watched Red Stang, the man who had cheated him of his vengeance. Stang's lips were moving, and occasionally he would gesture with his left hand, as though he were talking to someone, and explaining what had happened.

Jeff Dawson forgot his anger as he watched the tall redhead. He drew closer, and Stang heard the scuff of approaching boots. He stood up with his right hand close to his holster; relaxed when he recognized Dawson.

"Howdy, Red," Dawson said softly, and removed his hat.

"Did you follow me here?" Stang asked bluntly.

Dawson shook his head. "I come back here to talk to an old feller," he answered. "I wanted to tell old Jim that he could take his rest now that Terry Boyd is kicking up hot ashes in the Devil's coalpile!"

"Funny," Stang muttered. "Jim Dawson is resting right next to old Fred Haney. I was just telling old Fred."

"Haney has been dead three years," Dawson said tonelessly.

"Haney was an outlaw," Stang said slowly. "But old Jim saw that he got a decent burial."

"Old Jim was branded a lobo when we buried him here," Dawson said in a muffled voice. "You ever stop to think how things work out, Red?"

"I've done nothing else for three years," Stang answered. "The same side-winder did for both those old he's; they were both marked with the owl-hoot brand, and now they rest here together!"

"You worked for Terry Boyd," Dawson said musingly. "You tipped him off about me and Ben Stokes. Then you killed him!"

"I trailed that son for a year down in Texas," Stang said quietly. "I was riding behind the badge of a Texas ranger, like you know. I had to be sure!"

"Sure of what?" Dawson asked bluntly.

"Sure that Terry Boyd was the man I wanted," Stang answered sullenly. "He mixed with shady characters wherever he went, and they fleeced him at the gambling tables."

"Yeah, I know," Dawson agreed. "Tom and Dix Boyd were working hard on the 3 B, and Terry was spending more than they made!"

"He had plenty of money, and he borrowed even more," Stang explained. "When he finally quit Texas, I turned in my badge and followed him up here!"

"Why did you do all this?" Dawson asked curiously.

"I made a promise to an old feller," Stang muttered.

"To Fred Haney?"

"That's right," Stang agreed. "Haney came to me when I was just your age; just before I was twenty-one. Told me how come him to be tangled up with the James gang."

"I knew old Fred—that is, for a few hours before he went West," Dawson said gently. "I'd like to know."

"Seems like old Fred got drunk one night," Stang said gruffly. "He was drinking with a bunch of fellers who had plenty of money. They left old Fred outside a saloon to hold the horses. Then this gang robbed the saloon, and Fred had to ride with them!"

"When he sobered up," Dawson asked, "what did Haney do then?"

"They were back in the brush then," Stang explained. "The leader told Haney that the townspeople had recognized him holding the horses for a fast getaway. This leader was one of the James boys!"

"He joined the gang?" Dawson asked.

Red Stang frowned. "He couldn't quit," he said angrily. "After that, he always held the horses!"

"They held up the Katy Flyer down there in the Nations," Dawson said reminiscently. "They held up several other trains."

Stang nodded. "I know," he said gruffly. "That's when the law began to close in. Jesse James was killed by Bill Ford, and the rest of the gang rode their spurs up here and hid the loot. Old Fred Haney was with them at the time."

"Most of the gang was captured or killed," Dawson said quietly. "Where was old Fred all that time?"

"For two years he was back in the hills walking sheep," Stang answered, and his nose wrinkled to tell of his disgust. "Then he grew a beard, and he worked as a swamper in border saloons."

"He was a broken old man when he came up here," Dawson said reminiscently. "But there was still a lot of character about him, and plenty of fight!"

"He never had a chance to fight up here!" Stang said angrily. "He was set upon by those three and almost beaten to death!"

"I know," Dawson murmured. "I saw old Fred."

"Them three tried to make him tell where the loot was buried," Stang continued the familiar tale. "When he wouldn't talk, Terry Boyd killed him!"

"And you killed Terry Boyd," Dawson added.

"I killed him!" Stang admitted fiercely. "Just like I promised old Fred I would!"

"We've got a lot in common," Jeff Dawson said gruffly, and he stared hard at Red Stang. "I knew it this afternoon!"

"You knew what?" Stang demanded suspiciously.

"That you were kin to old Fred Haney!"

Red Stang whirled with a hand on his gun. "He wasn't no kin to me!" he denied. "Just an old saloon bum who got a bad deal!"

"Yeah," Dawson agreed. "So after he held those horses that first time down there in Texas, folks began to call you the Lobo's Whelp!"

Red Stang's six-shooter hissed against holster leather as the gun leaped to his right hand. He jammed the weapon in Dawson's belly, leaned against it with the hammer back, and stared hotly into Dawson's calm eyes.

"Unsay them words!" he demanded hoarsely. "Before I lean against the trigger!"

"You won't shoot," Dawson said quietly. "Old Fred was your dad, and we both know it. Old Jim was my dad, and I'm not ashamed of it!"

Red Stang glared and then stepped back. He holstered his pistol, turned his back, and sank down near the old grave.

"He was my old man," he whispered. "He came up here three years ago to find that loot. He was going to turn it over to the law, and take what they gave him. He never had a chance!"

"That's what old Jim aimed to do," Dawson said slowly. "I aim to do the same, if I ever find it."

Red Stang looked up and studied Dawson's bronzed face. "Is that on the level?" he asked sternly.

"I swear it, on the grave of old Jim!" Dawson said firmly, and his voice held a note of reverence.

"You'll take me in as pards on this new deal?" Stang asked hopefully. "To find that loot and turn it over to the law?"

"Here's my hand on it," Dawson answered.

Red Stang gripped the Triangle D cowboy hard. "I'll take the same swear on old Fred's grave," he promised in a husky whisper.

"Terry Boyd was part of the Stokes gang," Dawson told the tall redhead. He explained about the note Stokes had left in Gospel Cummings' cabin. "The same man wrote that note who wrote the one I found in my house," he added. "We better get back to let Gospel know you will stay for supper."

Red Stang looked at the grave of old Fred Haney, and put on his Stetson. He followed Dawson between the graves, and they entered Cummings' cabin together. The old plainsman smiled and pointed to the table where three places had been set.

"How'd you know I'd be here?" Stang asked.

"Knew you'd head back here to tell old Fred," Cummings said quietly.

Red Stang stared and then glanced at Dawson. Jeff smiled and nodded. "Don't forget that Gospel is the best sign-reader in these parts," he reminded.

"And don't forget that I knew old Fred when we were both yearlings," Cummings added. "You're the spitting image of him. Let's fly at those steaks before they get cold."

The three men ate in silence, each busy with his own thoughts.

"Old Fred came up here to find the loot," Cummings finally broke the silence. "I talked to him just before he died!"

Red Stang glanced up from his plate. "Did he tell

you where it was buried?" he asked breathlessly.

"Not exactly," Cummings said slowly. "But he knew about where to look. There was a big cave near a waterfall, between two low hills. A creek flowed along up above."

Jeff Dawson showed excitement. "There used to be a creek back there where—where Terry Boyd died," he said. "That creek has been dry for several years, but there used to be a small waterfall there, too!"

"Yeah, I know," Cummings murmured. "I didn't think the time was right to look for it."

"The time is right now," Dawson said with a smile. "I might have known you'd know more about it than you'd say."

"I wanted no part of it," Cummings said slowly. "I knew I'd never live to turn it over to the law if I made a search and found the loot. Terry Boyd would have bush-whacked me like he did them other two old mossy-horns, so I waited until some help came along."

"Jeff and I have made a deal, Gospel," Stang spoke up. "We want to find that loot and turn it over to the law!"

"Then you've got two partners," Cummings said with a slow smile. "Count me in."

"I don't want any part of that mouthy deputy!" Stang declared gruffly. "I won't work with him!"

"You mean you won't work with the law?" Cummings asked sharply.

"Not with Saint John!" Stang answered vehemently.

"The Saint don't lack none for cold nerve," Cummings said.

"That big son is all ankles and wrists!" Stang said angrily. "The Saint blunders around like an old range bull that has been whipped out of the herd. Like this afternoon when we had that Stokes gang under our guns!"

"There's other kinds of law," Cummings said quietly.

Red Stang tapped his holster. "I've got plenty of that kind right here!" he agreed.

Gospel Cummings frowned. "That kind of law has made an owl-hooter of many a good man," he said gruffly. "Now you take the best kind of peace officer; he does very little talking, but you can always depend on him in a pinch!"

"Like the Rangers," Stang insisted stubbornly. "You can mebbe so kill them, but you can't ever make one quit!"

"I know how you feel about Saint, but you could do worse," Cummings argued. "Now don't get me wrong," he said hastily. "You both heard what I told Saint John this afternoon. But he is the law, and he's got the cold nerve of the devil himself!"

"And just about as much sense," Stang said coldly.

Gospel Cummings frowned as he watched Stang's angry but determined face. Red drank his hot coffee and refused to meet the plainsman's eyes.

Jeff Dawson stared at the bearded face, trying to read what was going on behind those sorrowful brown eyes.

"You mentioned another feller," he said thoughtfully. "And you've been palavering about the law. You mean Charley Bailey?"

"Son, that's reading sign with the best!" Cummings said with open admiration. "When did you guess that Bailey was a law-dog?"

"I was sure of it today," Dawson answered honestly. "Charley wanted to get evidence, and he used to be a Texas Ranger. There's something about the way he looks at a man; something in the way he talks!"

"You mean Charley Bailey is riding behind a law-star now?" Stang asked slowly. "Did he tell you?"

Gospel Cummings shook his head. "He never said a word," the plainsman admitted. "But it all adds up!"

"But he wouldn't work with the Saint," Dawson reminded him. "And Saint John is the law in these parts!"

"And he's kinda noisy, like Red pointed out," Cummings explained. "There's only one kind of law-star Charley could be wearing. He's working for the Circle F, and he came up here from Oklahoma. Before that he was in Texas. What's your guess, Red?"

"United States deputy marshal," Stang said promptly. "Roving commission, or on a special assignment. He's out to recover that loot, and to nail the Stokes gang!"

"You and Jeff want to work with me and Charley?" Cummings asked with a little smile.

"That's good enough for me," Dawson agreed without hesitation.

"Suits me down to a gnat's eyelash," Stang said eagerly. "I rode with Charley many's the time down there in Texas. I should have figured him long before this!"

"Had me fooled," Dawson admitted honestly. "But I must have sensed it when I asked Ace Fleming to let Charley ride with me."

"And I was talking about Saint John being thick," Stang said, to show his disgust with himself. "I did have a hunch that Charley was after that treasure, but I didn't tag him as part of the law!"

"He almost talked out loud when he insisted that we all listen to get the evidence on Stokes and Terry Boyd," Cummings pointed out.

"I can see it now," Dawson murmured. "But then, a puzzle always seems simple when another feller has worked it out."

"Company coming," Stang said quickly. "Looks like old Cole Brighton and his pretty daughter!"

Jeff Dawson pushed back from the table and ran outside. He greeted the old cattleman warmly, and tipped his hat to Connie.

"I'll go in and talk to Gospel," Brighton said.

Connie dismounted, and Dawson tied up her horse. They walked across the yard toward the old barn, and sat down on a log.

"I'm glad, Jeff," Connie said in a whisper. "Glad you didn't have to keep your promise!"

"In a way, I'm glad too," Dawson agreed. "Being in love sotter changes a man in some ways."

"Are you in love?" Connie asked, and she watched Jeff with her red lips parted.

"I've loved the same girl for years, seems as though," Dawson whispered. "Thought about her all the time I was riding out back in the tangles. Some day I'm going to ask her to marry me, when this business is all settled!"

"I hope you will be very happy," Connie murmured. "Do you mind if I go and join my father?"

Jeff Dawson gasped, and then his arms went around Connie. "Please don't go now," he pleaded. "I love you so dad-burned much, I get all stuffed up inside!"

"Oh!" Connie murmured. "I didn't know it was me!"

Jeff Dawson tightened his arms. After a moment he raised his head from her blonde curls. "You knew all the time," he accused her gently. "I as good as told you so back in Lost River Cave."

"Yes, Jeff," Connie admitted. "But I wanted to hear you say it. Please say it, Jeff!"

226

"I love you, Connie," Jeff whispered. "When this ruckus is settled, and I'm of age, will you marry a poor cow-feller who is trying to get him a start in the cow business?"

"Oh, Jeff, darling, yes," Connie whispered. "It seems a year since we were together in that cave!"

For a long time there was silence. Then Jeff Dawson said in a whisper, "I'm going to ask Red Stang to be my best man!"

"I like Red," Connie agreed. "He's so much like you in so many ways. I've noticed his eyes when he didn't know anyone was watching. Like he was hiding something he was ashamed of."

"Yeah, Red is like me in some ways," Dawson said slowly. "You remember what they used to call me?"

Connie Brighton shuddered. "Let's not think of it," she whispered.

"They called Red the same thing, back in Texas," Jeff said soberly. "You see, old Fred Haney was Red's Dad!"

Connie caught her breath sharply. "Now I know why he killed Terry Boyd," she answered.

"You never can tell," Dawson murmured. "Tom Boyd and his brother Dixon are as honest as the day is long. Terry Boyd was a member of the Stokes gang!"

Connie grasped Jeff by the left hand. "Ben Stokes is still at large!" she said excitedly. "With two of his men!"

"That's right," Dawson agreed. "But they won't be for long," he added sternly.

"Promise me not to get into any more trouble," Connie pleaded. "Let John Saint John handle those outlaws."

Jeff Dawson sighed. "I've made an agreement," he said hesitantly. "With old Gospel, Red Stang, and Charley Bailey. We are going to hunt that gang down before Stokes finds the buried loot!"

"Must you?" Connie murmured. Then she changed and squeezed the cowboy's hand. "I know you will," she said proudly. "But do be careful, Jeff. We have waited so long!"

"We can wait a bit longer," Jeff said quietly. "There's two old fellers back there in the Devil's Graveyard who have waited even longer. Red and I both made them the same promise, and for now, they come first!"

Connie came closer and hugged Jeff tightly. "That's why I love you, Jeff," she whispered. "You won't ever betray a friend, or go back on a promise!"

"We better be getting back to the cabin, before old Gospel gets suspicious," Jeff suggested.

Gospel Cummings smiled when the young couple came into the cabin. Cole Brighton was smoking his old brier pipe, and he allowed the smoke to curl up over his head.

"When will you be of age, Jeff?" the old cattleman asked.

"In about three months, give or take a day," Dawson answered. "Any particular reason, old Cole?"

"Gwan," Brighton snorted. "You ain't fooling anybody, yearling!"

"I don't know what you mean," Dawson muttered, and his face flushed with embarrassment.

"I'll do it for you, pard," Red Stang added his bit. "Just tell me when."

"Bunch of comical hands," Jeff Dawson growled.

"Wait until you arc of age, and this thing is settled," Cole Brighton said pointedly. "You hear me, gal?"

"I didn't say anything, Dad," Connie protested. "We don't know what you are talking about, do we, Jeff?"

Jeff Dawson stared at the floor, raised his head, and squared back his shoulders. "Yes, we do," he said manfully. "And I'd be glad if we looked so happy that all the world could tell we're in love. Any of you characters want to make something out of that?"

"I do," Cole Brighton answered promptly, and he extended his right hand. "Let me be the first to congratulate you, my boy!"

"Gee!" Dawson blurted. "You mean it's all right with you and Ma Brighton for Connie and me to get married a bit later?" he asked hopefully.

"Right as rain, son!" Cole Brighton assured the

Triangle D cowboy. "But about this other deal; this is another round-up job for all the cattlemen in the Strip. The Boyd boys sent word over that they would be riding over tomorrow to help clean out the Stokes gang!"

CHAPTER SIXTEEN

Jeff Dawson sat up in his bunk in the Triangle D ranch house. Red Stang roused up in the bunk opposite. Both cowboys put on their Stetsons and stomped into their boots. After which they donned the balance of their range attire, neither man speaking.

The sun was just winking over the rim of Lobo's Peak. Dawson stirred cake batter, and lined the skillet with bacon. With the blackened coffee-pot on the back of the stove, and the fire going good, Dawson cleared his throat as he glanced at Red Stang.

"There will be Ace Fleming and part of the Circle F crew," he said slowly. "Cole Brighton and his Box B riders, and those fellers from the 3 B."

"So we'll get an early start like we agreed," Stang said slowly, but his voice told of his satisfaction with the arrangements. "I feel better than I have in years," Stang said quietly. "Something kept driving me so's I couldn't take my rest."

"I know what you mean," Dawson agreed. "I reckon we both found some measure of content last evening back there in Hell's Half Acre. Not only that, but Jim and old Fred will rest better now."

Half an hour later they mounted their horses and struck out, toward the northwest. They rode in silence until they reached the fringe of the badlands. Both reined their horses to a stop when a dull muffled boom echoed back from the distant foothills.

"Ben Stokes isn't losing any time," Stang said quickly. "And we better not lose any more!"

They followed the trail of the preceding day, but now they circled to the west of the two little hills, riding watchfully. They had talked over their plan, and each knew exactly what to do. This time they would come in to cut off the one avenue of escape which had been left open to Stokes and his henchmen when Charley Bailey had listened to get evidence.

A dust-and-smoke cloud hovered over the little depression between the two hills where the outlaw loot was thought to have been buried. The dust was settling as the two cowboys rode toward the place where a gang of desperate outlaws had hidden their ill-gotten gains.

Jeff Dawson knew every foot of the badlands from bitter experience. He took the lead and rode into a narrow defile, dismounted, and ground-tied his horse with trailing whangs for a fast getaway, in the event that one would be needed.

Red Stang followed Dawson's example, and both men loosened their six-shooters against crimp, after the long ride. Again Jeff Dawson took the lead and continued through the defile with Stang crowding his heels. Then they heard excited voices.

"The loot is here, Ben. Good thing we brought those gunny-sacks; these old saddle-bags are rotten!"

"That's Joe Stevens," Stang said huskily. "He had a hand in beating up old Fred!"

"Don't get to fighting your head," Dawson cautioned. "That ain't the law-way, pard!"

"It's better than any of them deserve," Stang muttered.

"I know, but that wouldn't get results," Dawson cautioned. "We don't want any of them to get away; we'll have to stick to the plan we made!"

The two cowboys crept forward and paused at the mouth of the defile. They could see the gaping mouth of a big cave where fresh earth had been blasted recently. The smell of black powder was strong in the morning air to tell of the explosion they had heard.

A man was standing in the entrance of the cave with his back to them. A tall lean man with the features of a hawk, and a brace of heavy six-shooters thonged to his sinewy thighs.

"That's Joe Stevens," Stang whispered.

He took a step to the left to thin the target they made. A small pebble rattled under Stang's boot, and Stevens whirled like a vicious cat. The tall outlaw's hands rapped down for his twin sixes, but Red Stang was already in action.

The ex-Ranger made his draw, thumbing back the hammer of his pistol on the up-pull. Orange flame belched from his right hand just as Stevens cleared leather with his pair of forty-fives.

Stevens was slapped into a turn as the heavy slug caught him in the left shoulder. He stomped his boot to stop the turn, and his right hand arced around with his six-shooter swinging for a target.

Jeff Dawson saw that murderous killer-gun swinging to center on Red Stang. Dawson triggered a shot even while Stang was notching back his hammer for a follow-up that would have been too late.

Joe Stevens grunted and went to his knees with both arms hanging limp at his sides. Dawson and Stang took to the brush like rabbits, one on each side of the trail, and a shot lashed the tall bracken just as Dawson made his dive to safety.

Red Stang answered the winking firefly that lanced from the interior of the cave. This gave Dawson time to change his position, and he sent three shots into the cave to seal off escape.

The echoes of the thundering guns died away in the low ring of hills. Two keen-eyed men watched the entrance to the cave, out in the early sunshine. Two trapped men stared at the light from the dark recesses of the musty old cave.

Jeff Dawson reloaded his six-shooter, and called guardedly. "Are you all right, Red?"

"They never touched me," Stang answered. "How about you?"

"All in one piece," Dawson whispered back. "I can't say the same thing for Stevens out yonder."

Joe Stevens groaned and sat up. "Stay back, Ben!" he shouted hoarsely. "It's Stang and Dawson, and I'm done for!"

"Crawl back in here!" Stokes shouted hoarsely.

"Stay where you are!" Stang said sternly. "Or I'll dot your squinchy eyes, you blasted owl-hooter!"

"I'm bleeding out," Stevens answered weakly.

"Crawl back here!" Dawson shouted. "I'll do what I can, but if your pards get Red, I'll smoke you down pronto!"

"Wait a minute, Joe!" Stokes shouted. "How bad you hurt?"

"Got a slug through both shoulders," Stevens answered weakly. "I'm losing a bucket of blood!"

"Crawl on out," Stokes gave grudging permission. "You'll stretch a new rope if the law gets you!"

Stevens staggered to his feet and came slowly down the trail. Red Stang watched the cave and spoke from the side of his mouth.

"Take care of him, Jeff; I'll see that Stokes and Cross stay put!"

"Up the defile!" Dawson shouted. "Stop around the bend!"

Joe Stevens started through the defile, went to his knees, and crawled around the bend. Dawson wormed his way through the brush and joined the wounded man.

"Red would have killed you yesterday," he told Stevens. "You had a hand in beating up old Fred Haney!"

"Plug up them holes," Stevens pleaded. "You can stop the bleeding!"

"I ought to let you bleed out," Dawson said harshly. "And you might see the time you will wish you had!"

"Why didn't you kill me?" Stevens snarled. "You had a free shot!"

"You remember Gospel Cummings?" Dawson asked. "Reckon mebbe I've been seeing too much of Gospel. He allows this sort of thing don't call for a killing!"

"Bridle the palaver," Stevens groaned. "Plug up those holes, and preach that sermon later!"

Jeff Dawson reached for his knife and cut away the blood-soaked shirt. He examined the ugly wounds in both shoulders; used bits of cloth from the prisoner's shirt-tail to fashion a pair of crude plugs.

Stevens winced and swayed from bullet-shock.

Dawson made a pair of cloth tourniquets, applied them above the brachial points, and twisted the tourniquets with short sticks.

"Get back up there where we can watch you," Dawson ordered the wounded man. "The law will be along pretty soon, and I want to talk some to your pards!"

"Ben won't ever give up," Stevens muttered.

Dawson helped Stevens to his feet and steered the outlaw toward the mouth of the defile. Stevens sat down in the grass and leaned heavily against a volcanic rock.

"Luck ran out," he muttered. "There's better than a hundred thousand in money, not counting a sack of jewelry!"

"You in the cave!" Dawson shouted. "Jeff Dawson speaking!"

"Keep on talking," Stokes answered sullenly. "We'll cut you and Stang in for half of the loot for a chance to ride on out!"

"I wouldn't trust you with snow-water, and let you melt it yourself!" Dawson answered. "Come out and surrender; we will guarantee you protection, and a fair trial!"

"Guess again!" Stokes sneered. "You were an owl-hooter yourself for three years. You and Stang want all the loot for yourselves!"

"Better surrender, Stokes," Stang called clearly. "All the cattlemen are headed this way, and every one of them carries a rope on his saddle!"

"They've got to catch us first," Stokes called derisively. "We'll take some of you along with us before we quit doing what we're doing right now!"

"Right now you are shaking in your boots," Stang retorted. "You know you don't have a chance, and both of you are afraid to die!"

"Try me," Stokes bellowed.

"Step out for a draw-and-shoot on an even break!"

"That was yesterday," Stang answered coldly. "I gave Terry Boyd an even break because I had it to do. And Terry Boyd is dead!"

"You ain't the law no more!" Stokes answered.

"Did you know old Fred Haney?" Stang asked.

"I knew that old swamper," Stokes answered. "He got drunk one night in Conestoga, and talked with his mouth wide open. Said he was coming up here to recover the loot, and turn it over to the law!"

"If that was good enough for him, it's good enough for me," Stang said clearly. "Fred Haney was my old man!"

There was a moment of silence while the two outlaws digested Stang's statement. Then Stokes said slowly: "No wonder you did for Terry Boyd!"

"One more thing, Stokes," Dawson said sharply. You wrote that note and left it in my house the day after old Jim was buried!"

"Not that it matters, but yore just guessing," Stokes answered.

"I'm not guessing," Dawson said positively. "It matched the writing you left down at Three Points in Gospel Cummings' cabin!"

"Did someone mention my name?" a deep voice asked, and the gaunt plainsman raised his head from the brush behind Red Stang.

"Gospel!" Dawson said jerkily. "I didn't hear you snaking your way through the grass!"

"So I noticed," Cummings agreed dryly. "You see, Jeff, I used to fight the redskins. I'm glad you and Red didn't kill Stevens!"

"Are you that old sin-buster?" Stevens asked hopefully.

Gospel Cummings frowned. "I'm the caretaker of Hell's Half Acre," he said with simple dignity.

"Give me a snort of snake-bite," Stevens pleaded. "I've lost a lot of blood!"

Gospel Cummings reached into the tail of his long coat, brought out a bottle and removed the cork. He held the bottle to the wounded outlaw's lips, and Stevens drank a deep draft.

"Builds a man up where he's all tore down," Stevens muttered. He regained some of his color, and his voice was stronger when he shouted at his companions in the cave.

"Better give up, Ben! Old Gospel Cummings is here, and the law won't be long!"

"Got your note, Stokes," Cummings called. "Thanks for the donation. Better come out with your hands up, you and Cross!"

"Go to blazes!" Ben Stokes shouted viciously, and three shots rattled from the cave to cut the brush above Joe Stevens' head.

Gospel Cummings was crouched to the side. His gun leaped to his big hand, and he spaced two shots between the fireflies which had winked out from the cave. A yell greeted his shots, and then there was a brooding silence which matched the sorrow in the plainsman's eyes.

"Better cave, and pitch your weapons out!" Cummings called sternly. "If the cattlemen get here they'll burn you out and kill you like rats. Better surrender now like men!"

"We can hold out till hell freezes over, and then skate on the ice!" Ben Stokes shouted. His gun blasted savagely, but the outlaw only wasted lead.

Gospel Cummings glanced at his companions. He smiled as the bullets raked the leaves above their heads, and his smile gave the two younger men an added confidence.

"It won't be long now," Cummings said quietly. "They'll cave before the sun goes down!"

"Don't shoot!" a voice called loudly. "One of your slugs creased Ben, and I'm coming out to surrender!"

Red Stang and Jeff Dawson crouched forward, six-shooters ready for war. Ad Cross appeared in the cave with his hands above his head. Dawson leaped to his feet and ran up the steep trail.

"Take care of Cross," he shouted at Stang. "I'll get Stokes!"

"Down, you fool!" Stang shouted. "That owl-hooter might be playing possum!"

Jeff Dawson heard the warning and he threw himself down, just inside the mouth of the cave. A gun roared thunderously, and a bullet whined above his head as Dawson hit the floor of the cave.

Dawson rolled over and triggered a slug at the flash of the bush-whack gun. He heard gun-metal thud to the floor, and then a voice spoke hoarsely.

"Don't shoot again, Whelp. I'm caving complete!"

"On your feet!" Dawson ordered sternly. "Walk out of the cave, or I'll finish what old Gospel started!"

"I'm coming out!" Stokes warned the men outside. "I'm wounded bad!"

Jeff Dawson's eyes had now shed the sunlight, and he saw Stokes approaching the mouth of the cave. Dawson got to his feet, stepped behind Stokes, and herded the wounded outlaw leader into the clear.

A trickle of blood ran down the outlaw's scalp to show where Cummings' bullet had creased his skull. His left arm hung at his side, and his right hand was shattered and bleeding from the bullet Dawson had fired at the flashing gun. Despite his wounds, Ben Stokes walked down the steep trail with no sign of fear. A group of horse-backers was racing up the east trail with Ace Fleming and Charley Bailey in the lead.

"Quite a party," Stokes said carelessly. "Well, I knew the rat-race would have to end some day."

"You'll hang when you heal up your hurts, Stokes," Dawson said heavily. "In a way, I'm sorry."

"Sorry!" Stokes growled. "If you was that sorry, you'd have called your shot better there in the cave!"

"I'm not a cold killer," Dawson answered, and he added, "In a way I'm glad I'm not!"

"Bridle your jaw," Stokes growled. "And don't worry about me dancing on air. I'm wounded bad, and I won't last long!"

Charles Bailey slid his horse to a stop, and took in the situation at a glance. He walked up to Ben Stokes and spoke sternly.

"You and your pards are under arrest, Stokes. Deputy U. S. Marshal Bailey speaking. Anything you say will be used against you!"

"Hawg-wash!" Stokes sneered. "I said it all the other day when you were listening, but I never figured you for the law-joker in the deck!"

"They are your prisoners, Marshal," Red Stang told Bailey. "Jeff and I want to take a look at that loot yonder. You don't mind?"

"Not a bit, Red," Bailey answered gruffly. "We'll be waiting for you."

Stang and Dawson walked up the steep trail

together, and into the mouth of the cave which had been sealed off for ten long years.

"The loot is yonder," Dawson said in a hushed voice.

They crossed the big cave together, and stood looking down on four old leather saddle-bags. The leather had rotted with age, and gold and paper money was spilled on the limestone floor. Dawson leaned down and prodded a chamois sack, and it burst to cascade a stream of flashing jewels on the floor.

"Two men died for this stuff," Jeff said slowly. "Your old man and mine!"

"They will sleep better now," Stang answered quietly. "They both wanted to turn that loot over to the law."

"If that was good enough for them, it suits us," Dawson murmured. "Chips off the old blocks!"

"Whelps, they called us both," Stang added. "But we rode on the right side of the law!"

"Yeah," Dawson agreed. "You'll be best man at my wedding, pard?"

Stang nodded his red head, and an expression of sadness crossed his thin young face. "And then I'll be drifting," he added.

"You don't like it here?" Dawson added.

"I like it fine!"

"Then buy in again and pardner me in the Triangle D," Dawson said quickly. "We can build a first-class spread in five years or so!"

"You mean it, Jeff?"

There was a happy lilt to the tall redhead's voice as he stared at his former partner. The years seemed to drop away from him, and he smiled happily when Jeff Dewson slowly extended his right hand.

"Never was more serious in my life, Red," Dawson assured Stang. "What do you say?"

"Cowboy, you've got yourself a partner!" Stang shouted.

He sucked in a deep breath, and offered his hand with a smile. "There's a little filly down in Texas," he admitted shyly. "We'll have us a double wedding, and I'll build a place on the Triangle D."

They left the cave without another look at the outlaw treasure, walked down the steep trail, and joined the party which now numbered a score of men. Red Stang spoke to Charley Bailey.

"The loot is all there in the cave, Marshal. Jeff and I want to turn it over to the law!"

"Spoke like a man, Red," Gospel Cummings praised Stang.

"Red and I are going to be pards in the Triangle D," Dawson announced. "And that ain't all of it. Red is going back to Texas to get the future Mrs. Stang. We're going to have a double wedding!"

Dawson walked back into the brush to get his horse, and Red Stang followed him. They caught their horses, and then rode away from the crowd.

"I've got to get back to Connie fast," Jeff told Red Stang.

"I want to stop in town and leave something with Fat Farrel for old Gospel," Stang said with a grin. "And I'll tell the world that if I'm just half the man old Gospel is now, when I'm his age, I won't ask for anything better!"

Jeff Dawson turned in the saddle. He waved his hand at Gospel Cummings, who answered with a wave of his old black Stetson.

"Let 'em go," Gospel Cummings told the smiling cattlemen. "But take a good look at a pair of men who have growed up fast. Seems only yesterday that we were calling Jeff Dawson the Lobo's Whelp!"

Charles M. Martin was born in Cincinnati, Ohio. In 1910 he worked for the California Land and Cattle Company. In 1915 he fought in Mexico as a mercenary soldier on the side of Pancho Villa. Later he worked on cattle ranches in various parts of the American West, sold paint products in Japan and China, was briefly a cowboy singer in vaudeville, and was a rodeo announcer in such places as Madison Square Garden in New York City and the Cow Palace in San Francisco. He began writing Western stories for pulp magazines in the early 1930s and continued to do so until the 1950s, something that in terms of his authentic background he was certainly capable of doing with a degree of verisimilitude. He published his first novel in 1936, *Left-Handed Law,* and followed it with *Law for Tombstone* (Greenberg, 1937). These novels introduced his character, Alamo Bowie, a Wells Fargo trouble-shooter and gunfighter. The character appealed to movie cowboy, Buck Jones, and both novels were made into motion pictures by Buck Jones Productions, *Left-handed Law* (Universal, 1937) and *Law for Tombstone* (Universal, 1937), with Buck Jones as Alamo Bowie. Martin was personally a brawling, hard-drinking individualist after the fashion of many of his fictional heroes. He carried on feuds with magazine and book editors as well as other writers. He worked so hard at his writing—at one time producing a million words a year for the magazine market—that on at least one occasion he suffered a nervous breakdown. In 1937 he began signing his name as Chuck Martin. He believed so passionately in the characters he was writing about that in the back yard of his home in southern California he created a graveyard for those who had died in his stories and by 1950 there were over 2,000 headstones in this private boothill. His stories always display great energy and continue to be read with pleasure for their adept pacing and colorful characters.

Center Point Publishing

600 Brooks Road • PO Box 1
Thorndike ME 04986-0001 USA

(207) 568-3717

US & Canada:
1 800 929-9108
www.centerpointlargeprint.com